PHILIPPA'S FLIGHT

Louise Couper

POOLBEG

A Note on the Author

Louise Couper was born in Dublin and graduated from Trinity College. She now lives with her husband and two sons on an organic farm.

Published 1997 by
Poolbeg Press Ltd,
123 Baldoyle Industrial Estate,
Dublin 13, Ireland

© Louise Couper 1997

The moral right of the author has been asserted.

The Publishers gratefully acknowledge the support of The Arts Council.

A catalogue record for this book is available from the British Library.

ISBN 1 85371 694 4

Cover painting by Stephen Darbishire
By Courtesy of Richard Hagen Ltd, Yew Tree House,
Broadway, Worcestershire WR12 7DT
Cover design by Poolbeg Group Services Ltd
Set by Poolbeg Group Services Ltd in Goudy 10.5/13.5
Printed and bound in Great Britain by
Cox & Wyman Ltd, Reading, Berks.

For Dublin
– where I was born

and

For Slieve Bloom
– where I found my inspiration

Also by Louise Couper

Philippa's Farm
Philippa's Folly

Published by Poolbeg

Chapter One

❧

I 'gin to grow aweary of the toil

"Glad to be back, Philippa?" Henry arrived breathless at my right cheek as I made my way to our beginning-of-term meeting.

"Of course." I lied. October is the worst time to begin a year, shrouded in mist and distinctly chilly. One can put up with almost anything on a sunny day but autumn has the hint of death in it. The death of hope? The death of love?

However, I kept all that to myself in case Henry thought I was disenchanted with my prestigious, poorly-paid position as senior lecturer in art history. He had one or two pets waiting in the wings, gown and mortarboard ready to hang on my personalised hanger.

He opened the door of the professor's office, only just enough, so that I had to press myself against him. Sadly, wide-brimmed hats and stiletto heels are no longer part of the female armoury.

"Ah, Miss Woodcock!" The prof, looking

resplendent in his burgundy jacket with the wine spills. "Come in, come in. Let us see what Rome and Florence have done to you."

I hoped it didn't show.

He peered over his half-moons and then at the list of publications on his desk.

"Well, Miss Woodcock, you scored a massive three articles!" he announced.

Henry smiled at me with a metaphorical thumbs-up. This is his way of trying to get inside my knickers. If it weren't for Eddie, I might let him – just to give him a slight shock.

"Ah. Yes. Here they are: *Aspects of Social Realism in Nineteenth Century Art* and *The Glorification of the Worker in the Nineteenth Century*. Highly interesting."

He never bothered to read them. He's an architecture man himself, all full-blooded columns and spatial excitement.

"And the next was *Light – the Discovery of the Impressionists*. Thought that one would have been done to death – shadows on snow and that endless lily pond series of Monet's. The man was obviously deranged."

"I suppose it will happen to us all. In time," I said, smiling.

"Very true, Philippa, very true," Henry rushed in. "Spot of tea, anyone?"

Boiling water was poured on to half a packet of tea leaves. Tea bags hadn't yet found their way into the hallowed precincts, still trapped in its eighteenth-century timewarp. However, feminism *had* raised its ugly head. I left the tea-making to the men – in case they thought it was a woman's job. But they got their own back with the biscuits. Always Mikado – those colourful abstractions of the female organ designed by a pervert. Henry gave me his usual knowing wink as he offered them. I refused and took one of the chocolate truffles from my briefcase.

After tea, the real business of the meeting was attended to – holidays: dates and times. The students we were supposed to be imbuing with wisdom and knowledge were merely incidental, unless they were exceptionally good or exceptionally bad. The middle stream were barely noticed. Except for Henry. He embosomed those who were well-fleshed. Unfortunately for the poor things, they seemed to enjoy it.

"Two important announcements before we disperse to our various sanctuaries," the professor said, putting his spectacles carefully into their case. "One, the new Dean of Art History is to be announced shortly and two, the French Department have managed to hijack Ionesco. This represents a certain coup. Do you think we could manage something? Anyone got an "in" with someone famous?"

"Well, unfortunately, Gandon and Palladio are out of town," Henry attempted levity and failed. As usual. He composed himself and creased his brow. "But perhaps we could persuade de Blacam & Meagher to visit."

"De Blacam & Meagher? I'm not quite *au fait* with

them – I've spent the summer in Roundstone. Perhaps you could enlighten me over a glass of Madeira."

Not all the Madeira in Christendom could enlighten the poor old professor.

Henry and I said good-bye as he dived into the common room for his glass of Madeira with the professor and I sought Bewley's, for an expensive, though peaceful, cup of tea.

Eddie was waiting for me. *Plus ça change* . . .

"Well, how's old Bonkers?" Eddie enquired.

The professor had been christened Christopher Goodbody – hence *Bon Corps*, or Bonkers. Most of academia's brainpower is taken up with creating nicknames.

"Usual old self. Seems he spent the summer in Roundstone. Not for him the dizzy heights of St Peter's or the Palladian splendour of the Tuscan hillsides."

"A trifle cynical on the first day of term, are we?"

Eddie himself looked the same as usual – archaeological but interesting, sad but witty.

"Let's hope it passes. I can't go through the whole year feeling like this. Maybe it's the weather."

"Let's go and see the new play in the Abbey, Pips. Maybe that'll cheer you up."

"No, Eddie. What I'd like to do is go through my notes, do some work on my thesis and get to bed early."

"That sounds even better."

"Alone."

"Oh."

Eddie lived in the anticipation of catching me in a weak moment and raising me to dizzy heights. However, archaeologists are preoccupied with the dead, perhaps not the best training ground for a sensational lover. And, at my age, one gets choosy.

"Wonder if Peaches would care to see a play . . ." Eddie said as he left the room.

This was designed to make me jealous. Peaches is the department secretary and, though she has the body of a Versace model, I've a suspicion she prefers women.

I worked through my timetable and organised the material for my lectures. Much the same as last year, except that I had more information to add and a new batch of slides, acquired with a great deal of trouble and expense, what with bribing museum attendants to turn a blind eye to my flashbulb and calling at the most obscure hide-aways of the rich who kept famous paintings in their basement. I always kept a can of hairspray handy in case of trouble. I needn't have bothered. Most of the seriously rich are either so fat they can barely reach the loo in time, or in such an advanced stage of decay that "boo" would scare the living daylights out of them.

The notes for my magnum opus, *The Struggle for Self-expression in Nineteenth-Century Art*, lay in piles wherever there was a blank space. I hadn't thought about it all summer long. Avoiding it, probably. I had a feeling that something was missing. My recurring dream was of drawer upon drawer of yellowing manuscripts which went blank as soon as I tried to read them. But finish it I had to. Just so that I could live comfortably with myself.

A knock on the door.

"OK for O'Dwyer's tonight, my sweet?"

Henry, trying to smile his most alluring.

"Not exactly the first thing on my agenda." Or even the last. I was determined to avoid the usual first of term booze-up, if at all possible.

"You simply must come tonight to meet our new member of staff. The Italian Renaissance replacement."

I remembered now. Poor old Mrs ffrench had a leg amputated during the holidays. Gangrene. Too much gin and fags. Bonkers said her tin leg on the stairs would disturb the peace. They were busy teaching her macramé.

"What's our newest recruit like?"

"Proustian."

Henry read my raised eyebrow; not such a low-watt bulb, at times.

"Well, you know, all sort of ephemeral and . . . you know . . . slim."

Indeed. I could hardly wait.

O'Dwyer's was typical of student haunts – dirty, crowded and depressing. Since lecturers are merely students who haven't managed to move on into the real world, we haunted the joint too.

Proustina was there before me, close by Henry.

"This is eh, Constantia. Philippa Woodcock – specialises in nineteenth-century painting."

Her smile was disarming, a beacon in the black abyss of the artfully-placed baby curls around her forehead.

"Heard so much about you, Philippa," she said, curls aquiver. "A fellow at twenty-four!"

I could have killed Henry. Nothing more guaranteed to dim one's achievements than to have them thrown at your face in a pub.

"Handy getting the free room at the time. The stock exchange was doing badly," I replied.

Henry brought the drinks. A pint of Guinness for Proustina, a man's drink – just to pretend she wasn't all curls and Brussels lace. One of those who actually enjoyed pelvic floor exercises.

"Constantia is Early Renaissance."

So that explained the Pre-Raphaelite mien.

"Lots of trips to Italy – though all that pasta and Chianti get a little tiring," I said by way of conversation.

"I hear you saying you don't like pasta and Chianti. Too bad."

Not another one who'd done a counselling course! They were supposed to learn how to listen but what they really taught was how to get one's retaliation in first, with a wet fish.

"I gather you adore pasta and Chianti. Good for you!"

Henry went to fetch another drink. He was really developing a problem.

Proustina made short work of the second burnt hops

7

and delicately wiped her mouth on the back of her hand. Definitely not *premier tiroir*.

"Well," said Henry, raising his glass and staring at me, "here's to another interesting and fulfilling year."

I presumed he meant he *hoped* it would be like that. If it was anything like last year, we might as well stay sozzled forever. Endless meetings, an amputation and a student who died of AIDS. Madly, madly gay. I showed my usual forbearance and didn't say a word.

A small man in a white jacket wandered towards us with half a platter of cocktail sausages. Henry gave his usual little boy smile and lifted a bundle. Proustina shovelled one into her mouth and took another. So precious and artistic, yet she needed to eat! She'd be off to the loo next.

"Thought we'd find you here, all snug – and gobbling too!" Professor Bonkers put a soft fat hand around my waist.

Poor Mrs Bonkers died tragically in the Venetian floodwaters desperately trying to save a Caravaggio. I had a soft spot for the widowed prof – though I wasn't sure where. I ordered a port and brandy for him and a plate of sausages.

"And how was Roma, m'dear?" he asked me, noisily grabbing air between sausages and brandy and port.

"Hot, but wonderful. I spent a week with the Fra Angelicos in the Vatican and climbed Bramante's Dome – at last."

Helped by large libations of Chianti and the

moustached curator of the Farnese. But this lot wouldn't understand.

"Quite a sight, quite a sight! Matilda and I did it all, but that was a long time ago."

Proustina pulled back her lips to reveal a perfectly white set of teeth that curved at the bottom like a tiger's claw. "You sound very wistful, Professor. It must be sad to be on your own."

"Well, to be perfectly honest," the prof sucked his lips and took a deep breath, "Marks & Sparks dinners certainly pall after a year or two."

Such is undying love – a warm bed and well-cooked dinner. Makes you want to fall in love with a poodle. At least it would pine over your grave.

"She used to make a beautiful apple crumble, did old Tillie," he said. His glazed eyes looked longingly into Proustina's. "Almonds in the topping."

No one could replace her in other words. One of those bossy little women who lorded it over their partners with a hot dinner. And cold bed.

Glasses were replenished for a third time. I was wondering why I was still there. Cold flat? My book lost its appeal? First day of term blues? Yet there was something familiar about it, a promise of something in the air which you could get if you only knew how to ask for it.

"You missed it, Pips." Eddie arrived, looking sparkling and full of himself. I felt like stamping on his toe. No one ever has the decency to be as miserable as oneself.

"Oh, the play!" I said nonplussed. "What was it?"

Peaches joined us.

"*Hell is Other People,*" he replied, putting a proprietorial arm around Peaches's pale shoulders. Her skin was blue with goose-pimples. The way people suffer to be beautiful! And her shoes were pinching her. I pulled out a stool.

"Thank you, Philippa." Respectful, anyway. Maybe she fancied me. "How's the work going? Having a publication deadline spoils the fun a bit."

Too true.

"Oh, I don't know. Original research and all that, clearing the academic cobwebs."

"Yours is about art and suffering, isn't it?"

"Not quite. More about expression – which should include joy, too." Though I wasn't sure I'd know that if it jumped up and bit me.

"I could tell you all about suffering. From the year dot," she said, knocking back the cider like it was lemonade. "I have suffered. I'm sure it began in my mother's womb. She really didn't want me – tried a gin bath and it didn't work. Probably why I can't stand the stuff."

She nodded at Eddie for a refill. Her long thin fingers extricated a bag of loose tobacco and a cigarette paper. Shred by shred, she placed the tobacco on the paper, up and down, nudging it into submission. Then she licked an edge and, with one of those movements that looks so easy but comes from years of practice, she rolled the cigarette like a pencil and sealed it. She coughed at the first puff.

"Lack of oral satisfaction as a child, they say," she said, puffing gallantly, though her eyes were bulging.

"At least you're getting it now," I said.

"Yes, but I'm killing myself in the process," she wheezed.

I could think of more exciting ways to go. Even Proustina seemed half normal in comparison. I made the mistake of looking in her direction.

"What do *you* think, Philippa? We were talking about Classicism versus Romanticism. I've been saying that the former is about emotion in a controlled state, whereas the latter is about unbridled passion."

She looked as though she knew all about that – from the television.

"For me," I said, as I took a breath and tried to be my most tolerant, "there is a coldness about Classicism which the Romantics tried to redress. After all, we're not just a brain – some aren't even a brain, of course – we have feelings, too."

Everyone stared into space or into their glass. I really ought to see about that poodle. Perhaps a tortoise would be easier to look after; they sleep for six months of the year.

Another drink was placed beside my still-full glass. They seemed to be springing up like triffids. Perhaps if we all got stewed, we wouldn't really notice what was happening. Later there would be the hangover, more punishment for having punished yourself in the first place.

Tiger Teeth was now flashing her fangs at Eddie.

"Archaeology, isn't it?" she encouraged, crossing her legs towards him.

"Greek and Roman mainly, but anything considered," Eddie replied, emphasising the "anything". I suddenly thought: was I "anything", too?

"And how do you feel about the reinterpretation of the old world in the eighteenth century?"

"Whatever turns you on, so long as you don't for a minute pretend it's anything but an imitation."

"Oh, it was much more than mere imitation. I did say reinterpretation." The fangs flashed.

"You would, wouldn't you, or you'd be out of a job."

Eddie was being his usual facetious self. A spoilt child, always looking for attention. Tiger Teeth was beginning to bristle. The tiny black hairs on her upper lip stood to attention like a *chevaux de frise*. She turned to Henry for some moral support but Bonkers was busy giving him a tin ear.

"They're only pictures, after all," I said, bringing things back to their essentials. It's these sorts of arguments that cause people to lob missiles at each other and become the best of friends again after their countries are reduced to rubble.

Peaches was busy lighting another cigarette with the remains of the old one. She edged closer to me.

"*That* one should try a day behind a typewriter. But it would be too lowly for *her*. Miss High-and-Mighty. Bet she had her parents robbed with getting grinds at school just so she could be better than anyone else.

And she hasn't a clue. Can't spell for toffee. Wrote Donatello with one 'l'."

One way to make life miserable was to tramp on the department secretary's corns. Documents get mislaid and important messages forgotten. I bought Peaches a large pint.

"I probably take my work too seriously. But knowledge is important, for its own sake." Tiger Teeth took up the cudgels once again.

I tried to stifle a yawn and failed. Henry edged closer to her while Bonkers took off for the loo.

"Well, an early start for me in the morning," I said to all and sundry. "But don't let me break up the party." I ordered another drink for everyone and left.

The night was foggy and chilly. I felt the usual sense of unreality as the cool air hit me. Elated, yet depressed at the same time, as if one half of me were in heaven and the other in hell.

It was too late for a bus, so I walked to Donnybrook. A bit daring. "Always look as though you'd explode if someone so much as said hello," Mother used to advise. She had no problem doing that. It was her *modus operandi*, even with the postman. Father used to pretend he didn't notice, as if nothing could be more natural than her hectoring and bullying.

"Do you think so, dear?" he used to say after one of her more aggressive outbursts. A wonderful ability to filter the tone and merely pay attention to the words. Would that I were so adept.

By the time I reached the end of Waterloo Road, I had sobered sufficiently to need a loo desperately. The Burlington was near, but a lone female at this time of night would be misinterpreted. A few steps down Morehampton Road and my bladder had had enough. It emptied in rivulets down my legs and into my shoes. Nothing like having a gay old time first day of term. Fortunately, my tights were black and home was merely ten minutes away.

Wet and cold I squelched my way to the cocktail cabinet. I made myself a stiff drink with the dregs of the sloe gin and some cherry brandy, and ran the bath. Every stitch into the washing machine. No sooner had I descended into the warm bubbles than the phone rang. It could only be bad news at this time of night. There are those who can leave a phone ringing. My curiosity always got the better of me.

"Thank God you're in!"

Agatha, my one and only sister. I should have stayed longer at the pub.

"I've lost it."

"It?" I was certain it wasn't her virginity.

"My ring, my antique diamond ring that nice man I met in Saudi Arabia gave me."

"That's hard luck," I said sincerely.

"It's probably been stolen," she shrieked. "These people I'm working with are peculiar, to say the least. Steal the winker off a nightmare. Whispering in corners all the time."

Probably chatting about our Ag and *her* peculiarities.

"I suppose I can kiss the ring goodbye. Claim on the insurance."

"I suppose that's it."

"Sorry to have bothered you, Philly. Just needed to hear a kindly voice."

Nothing about what my first day of term was like, how the book was going. Agatha was nothing if not consistent in her self-centredness. Bad enough pissing on yourself but to have your own sister do it too . . . Life could only get worse.

Chapter Two

❧

Death lays its icy hand on mothers . . .

Front Square was alive with little groups of Freshers, huddling together for comfort in their new, strange world. Earnest and wiser Sophisters were trying to persuade them to part with their money by joining the Phil and Hist, the Photographic Soc or, heaven forfend, the Boat Club. The important thing was to get the money for the free wine and burnt sausages which the permanent members were looking forward to, in the indisputable knowledge that ninety per cent of those signing on would never appear on the society's doorstep. Tours of the libraries were taking place, maps of the lecture theatres distributed. All different to my day when you had to fend for yourself, when part of the joy was actually finding yourself in the right place at the right time.

A room in Rubrics came with my job as senior lecturer. Tiny and cold but full of light with a view of New Square on one side and Library Square on the other. Half my time was spent watching the world walk, crawl or slither by.

I pulled myself back to the letter I was writing in order to avoid looking at my notes. I had forgotten where I had ceased in my meanderings and guesswork. Why couldn't the summer be longer?

Dear Mary

Will be in gay Paree in February – if I survive that long! Thanks for the offer of a bed – even if it's only a mattress. Please thank Monsieur and Madame also – I'll try not to eat them out of house and home. Will be happy to bring some decent tea – and jelly.

Regards,
Philippa

Mary Costello had gone to Paris the same time I was offered my lecturing job.

"I want a break from all that mind-boggling stuff in books," she'd said, "do something useful for a change like scrub a floor or wash curtains."

She was now on her fourth *au pair* job in three years. The main difficulty was the husbands.

"Fat, bald and stinking of garlic," Mary said; "They throw themselves at you and expect you to be thrilled."

"What happens if you meet one you actually, you know . . . fancy?" I asked.

"That's a bridge I'd be only too happy to cross when

17

I come to it," she replied, tossing her blond curls in the air as if shaking off the possibility.

I gathered my notes on the Barbizon School for my first lecture of term and looked out the slides to match. I had ceased up-dating my notes and pictures after my first term when I discovered that half the students were asleep anyway, a quarter were missing and the remaining few were happy just to get the bare bones. Lucky to meet one student per year who was actually interested in the subject. Most were there to fulfil Mummy or Daddy's dreams or "pick up" a degree.

Eddie waved at me from the path below the window. The signal for coffee time.

"Within the walls or without?" he asked, rubbing his hands in anticipation. I knew he preferred Bewley's to anywhere.

"Perhaps we should give ourselves a treat, seeing it's our first day back in harness," I said, making for Front Gate.

It was always a shock to come into the noisy traffic and crush of pedestrians after the cocoon of College. We crossed at the lights and went towards Westmoreland Street.

"Think I'll have a bite to eat."

Poor Eddie was always hungry, not necessarily for food, though food often fitted the bill.

I had decaffeinated coffee – the real thing gets me over-excited – and an almond bun.

Little grey-suited twerps of about twenty buzzed about us, either answering their mobile phones or gesticulating wildly as their coffee got cold.

"Peaches get home OK?" I asked, pretending to be busy with my almond bun.

Eddie gave me one of his odd looks, where he twists up his mouth and screws his eyes almost shut like a blind ferret.

"She's a gay person; I mean a *real*, paid-up member of the ladies-only club."

I said nothing.

"You knew," he said, bending towards me. "And don't pretend otherwise. Nothing escapes you, Philippa."

"Very little." Unfortunately.

"Suppose I'm wasting my time asking you out tonight?"

"Afraid so, Eddie. It's my first lesson in macrobiotic cooking. A very *ancient* regimen. I thought maybe a change in diet would induce a change in consciousness."

"Really? You know, I'm sure there's a thesis or at least an article on the effect diet had on man. The explanation as to why some races are small and others tall. And size becomes a determinant for survival."

"Hardly anything new in that, Eddie. Even I know the reason the Chinese are small is due to a poor protein diet, and every schoolgirl knows the Vikings were tall because they had to get as much sunlight as possible to synthesise vitamin D."

He saw through me. There was only one fly on Eddie.

The course on macrobiotic cookery was better than any diet – the mere look and smell of our efforts would have put you off food for life. The only thing that kept me together was the thought of a juicy sausage sandwich with the butter dripping down my arm when I got home. However, on the doorstep lurked a dark, familiar shadow.

"Afraid I've had a trying evening, Eddie," I warned him and opened the door into the flat, the basement of a neo-Georgian edifice with garden front and back.

"That makes two of us." He followed me in without a by-your-leave. "I've had a gun put to my head to have my thesis in by Christmas. Sorry, Pips, just needed a shoulder to cry on."

I was under the illusion it was other parts of my anatomy he valued.

"What about Peaches?" I suggested softly. "She seems sensible enough."

"Not what you'd call 'warm'."

"So, it's really sex you want."

Important to get the lines cleared from the beginning.

"Never known to refuse – if that's an offer."

"Afraid not. The corn muffins did for me. Put you off living, never mind sex."

"Oh?"

"Chewing them saps every ounce of your energy."

"Well, maybe a cup of tea then."

The "real thing". I couldn't wait.

My two o'clock seminar was as exciting as usual. Eight out of fourteen turned up. One of the students who was to prepare a two-page essay on the Barbizon School hadn't bothered to get out of bed. This left the rather earnest Miss Rosalind Richmond-Quinsy to take the entire matter on her ample shoulders. Her two-page essay had approximately eight pages of notes and appendices. She insisted on going through the lot. As her deep voice droned on and on, a dark, Italian-looking student fell fast asleep on my couch. I noticed Miss Sorrel take advantage of his state by leaning against his legs. At her age, I might have been tempted too. However, one soon learns that good looks have nothing to do with it. "Tous les chats sont gris dans la nuit." He probably preferred men.

Undaunted by the air of post-prandial somnolence, Miss Richmond-Quinsy continued: "While Millais' *Gleaners* looks patronising and unrealistic, it is obvious . . ."

"Patronising?" I interrupted. It was important that students got the correct angle on things.

"Why, yes, Miss Woodcock. The rounded shapes, the drab clothes, the obvious routine of the work, as if they were made for it."

What about their dignity, their monumentality? Should I tell her or not? Was this what the job was about? Was there a "correct" way of looking at art?

I looked around the rest of the so-called seekers

after knowledge. Boredom, doodling, embarrassment and shyness oozed from every pore. Was it for this I had sought the groves of academe?

Miss Richmond-Quinsy sat resplendent in her red tapestry skirt and lace blouse, unchallenged and smug. I couldn't decide which was worse.

When they left, I made myself a cup of tea and put on Mozart. I searched through my collections of pictures and looked at *The Gleaners* bending to their task, collecting every stray length of corn, wasting nothing. I felt guilty that, in the midst of plenty, there was so much waste while others bent and lifted and sifted through acres of ground for a handful of seed. Was there anything to be gleaned from giving seminars to people who didn't care? Was I merely time-serving? Earning money to buy a bagful of groceries? I looked again at the gleaners, close to the earth, in tune with the seasons. Was such a life a possibility?

A knock on the door.

"Eddie!"

"I know. Oh, Pips, dreadful news – Mummy has just died! And you never even met her."

Perhaps that was a blessing for both of us.

"I suppose you'd better come in."

I refilled the still-warm kettle and wordlessly handed a very quiet Eddie his tea and offered the remains of last weekend's baking from my Italian biscuit barrel. He burst into tears.

"Sorry, Ed, it's all I've got."

He dragged his wet nose along his sleeve.

"It's not that! It's Mummy. She's dead."

Perhaps something with a bit of an anaesthetic was called for.

"Was she old?" I asked, pouring water on to some Scotch Agatha thought she'd hidden.

"Age has nothing to do with it!"

With such anger can sorrow be far behind?

"Sorry, Pips. I just wish she had chosen some other day to kick the bucket. I wasn't really ready for it. And now it's funerals and coffins and earth and sandwiches and all those awful relations I haven't seen since Aunty snuffed it."

"Strange how death is the one thing that brings everyone together."

"Maybe there's safety in numbers."

"Here, the hot Scotch will help. Sorry I haven't any crisps."

Eddie's favourite snack is Scotch and half a dozen bags of crisps.

"Maybe you'd nip out and get me a packet?"

His eyes looked so pleading, how could I refuse?

Bonkers waddled his way down the square in my direction. He spotted me before I had time to run for cover.

"Had a gorgeous lunch. Good old Henry and that nice Miss Constipation or something. Looks a bit like a pre-Raphaelite maiden, all flowing hair and garments."

More like Mary Magdalen before her conversion.

"You'd a good lunch, anyway," I said, edging my way to turn right for the shop.

23

"At least I didn't have to cook it," he said, his eyes watering just enough to grab the heart-strings. "I hear you're a dab hand at some newfangled cookery. Happy to help you with the nut cream if you make the apple crumble." He winked and lifted his tweed hat in farewell.

There might be life in the old man yet. I'd better make sure there was an army of boy scouts handy, just in case. Perhaps it wasn't only the food he missed.

Eddie was halfway through a bottle of St Emilion I was saving for a late-night dive into my research. I said nothing.

"Sorry, Philly. Swallowed the Scotch without noticing. Like some?"

He must have interpreted my body language. Some archaeologists notice the living, too.

I took out a glass and had a good mouthful. Nectar. A good wine seeps into every pore and makes one tingle.

"Can't let you swig the lot and be sick." I refilled the glasses.

"Why do we have to die, Philly? It's so final, so unfair."

Strange attitude from one who made his living from the dead. But there was no point in spoiling his little moan. Life offers few opportunities to indulge oneself.

"You could spend your whole time being good and you still end up the same as everyone else." He slugged back my wine as if it were water and helped himself to more.

"Poor Rennick from History dropped like a stone on the squash court. He barely had time to bid farewell to life and his partner, before breathing his last. The man had a resting pulse of 64, a cholesterol level of 4.6 and the best squeeze to his heart a body could have."

"My dear Eddie, perhaps he was miserable in his healthiness. Sadness kills just as merrily as a dicky heart."

"You should have studied psychology, Pips. You seem to have such insightful insights."

"Trouble is," I said, pouring the last of the wine into my own glass, "it's rats and pigeons you're expected to have the insights about. It's all so 'scientific' that an insight is heresy. Give me a good book any day. All the humanity you need."

I was so thoroughly depressed I decided to open the Chianti Classico I'd been keeping – for what, I couldn't remember. What I did remember was Eddie's hot breath coming in short pants and that warm, all-over pattern that only an orgasm can create. One of the nicest things about Eddie was his aftershave – patchouli. The sort of smell a girl would do anything for. Almost. I often wondered what precognitive experience it was tied up with for me. Perhaps mother rubbed it on her armpits and it wafted down to me as I sucked on the breast, or perhaps it was the smell from father's fishing tackle box . . .

I awoke at six o'clock with a cold bottom and sore head. The couch is not the most comfortable place, even with a Chianti anaesthetic. I extricated myself from Eddie's clutches and put the kettle on.

My notes stared up at me accusingly. *The Gleaners* would have cleared several fields in the time I had spent snoring my head off. Van Gogh would not only have chopped off another ear but painted it as well. I gathered up the notes and took myself to the table at the window. Proustina and Henry were down in the square, eyeball to eyeball, Proustina flashing the molars for all she was worth. Quite an art. There was an initial slight parting of the teeth, an infinitesimal spreading of the lips and then, wham – the sun came from behind the cloud, lips were pulled back like taut reins and the teeth shone like beacons. It must have taken her hours before a mirror. It was all wasted on Henry. He adores his wife and twin girls to distraction.

A groan from the couch. "Yuck."

"Tongue about ten sizes too big, head like a crushed melon? Don't tell me, Eddie. I've got the certificate."

"Bloody hell! Look at the time! I've missed Mummy's removal!"

"For goodness' sake, it's not that bad! I'm sure she got there OK. There's always the funeral . . ."

"But Ophelia will be in a tizwas – Mummy would have been really cross."

"Well, Eddie, I think your mother is really past caring. Now. And your sister is probably wise to your little peccadilloes. So, just get your glad rags sponged and pressed and you'll be fine."

"Pips . . . you wouldn't do something really laudable and unselfish for a good friend?"

"Seldom. There isn't an ounce of either in my bones."

"Not even if they promised a good supper and an escort to the "invitation only" Houshiari exhibition afterwards?"

"Well, that's different." A girl likes her sacrifices to be appreciated.

"I'll pick you up at nine in the morning."

I dragged out my funeral outfit – black crêpe over silk. It clung to every curve and sinew and flowed like water. Eddie gave me one of those looks, complete with dilated pupils, but I threw on my fur-lined cape and made for the door.

We were early; only the corpse was there before us.

"Popular – your mother?" I whispered, casting a glance at the coffin. It was too much for Eddie.

"Imagine Mummy's in that box! Dead."

Well, we could but hope it wasn't a pile of stones or someone's dead father. Perhaps there was a market in corpse-swapping. Did anyone ever check? However, I didn't plague him with my hang-ups and squeezed his leg instead.

"How can you, Philippa – with Mummy there?"

I felt like yelling it wasn't a come-on and, anyway, Mummy had better things to do, like get out of purgatory. However, I watched the priest on the altar lighting the candles instead and tried to count the number of angels that danced on the candle's flame. At least thirty-three – which was as far as I'd got when Eddie began to cry.

"I should have been better to her. I should have called more often, brought her out. Bought her better birthday presents."

"Would she have liked that?"

"No. She hated going anywhere. Couldn't stand people. Hated getting presents."

Sounded charming.

"Well, Eddie, I can't see what you have to reproach yourself with."

"But I should have tried harder. Made more of an effort."

A parent's legacy is guilt.

There was the tap of shoes on the church tiles. A large woman dressed in red clasped Eddie's hand and shook her head knowingly.

"She wasn't the worst," she said. "Did a lot for the V de P."

Eddie gave me a look. "That would be bloody typical. Give to strangers rather than her family."

I was in danger of feeling sorry for him. Pity's the slippery slope. Women mistake it for love when it's merely the maternal juices being stirred.

A few more bunches of people turned up and the priest appeared on the altar. The organ rumbled and a sound of such purity filled the space that I was almost moved. The *Ave Maria* brought tears to my eyes, and by the time *Panis Angelicus* arrived we both crumpled.

"Where on earth did you get such a singer?" I asked Eddie.

"That's Ophelia. Took it up after she had a hernia operation." He blew his nose into a lump of orange loo paper. "She used to warble a bit at home. Drove us all mad. Didn't seem to put her off."

The resilience of human nature. One can kill anything except talent.

I glanced to see if Eddie showed some sign of regret for his sibling nastiness but his tears were for himself only. As we stood to follow the coffin, *Dominus regit me* was whispered on the air. I looked up at the singer in the gallery. A female version of Eddie. She stood like a tree, arms outstretched, her voice echoing in the empty space.

"Amazing she can sing at her own mother's funeral," I burst out, unable to contain my wonder.

"She nursed Mummy at the end. I suppose she's relieved it's all over," Eddie said, dipping a finger into the holy water font as he passed, stray drops trickling down the side of his trousers.

"I'm not up to the planting just now, Eddie," lily-livered, I confessed. "Meet you in the Pig's Head whenever it's over."

I walked briskly away, in case Eddie's hangdog look got the better of me and I found myself tossing clay on to a coffin. Bad enough when you had to do it for your own relations.

I ordered a hot whiskey, complete with cloves and lemon from a, thankfully, mute boar. Small talk should be outlawed, like henna hair dyes. Pubs are for floating the mind, or whatever, not for anchoring it in reality.

The stalwarts nursing pints of Guinness slid sidelong glances towards me from beneath their manky hair. The smell of unwashed bodies was pervasive. A chicken sandwich would be an open invitation to join Eddie's mother.

"And some peanuts," I gestured towards the few remaining kippered packets. The boar tossed them to me and grunted for money.

The church bell announced the end of the ceremony. The pint drinkers rubbed their heads and took a long slurp. I made my way to a grimy window. Eddie's sister was coming down the steps with a familiar figure. Peaches. They briefly held hands and then Ophelia gave Peaches a hug, loosening Peaches's combs in the process, allowing her straw-coloured hair to fall around her face. Gently, Ophelia gathered it up and re-inserted the combs with practised ease.

Halfway through my third whiskey, Eddie put his head inside the Pig's. Not a happy head.

"Thanks for your support and all that. Just when we need our friends, they prefer to sit in a pub getting quietly sozzled with a bunch of stinking swine."

I hardly noticed the smell now. Too full of lemon and cloves, no doubt.

"Really, Philippa. It would be nice if you felt the teeniest bit guilty. Sometimes I think the only person you really like is yourself."

Eddie was perfectly entitled to his little rant and rave. He'd just buried his mother.

Two steaming glasses arrived. Mr Pig grunted, was paid and trotted off.

"You know I *hate* cloves. Who on earth thought the rest of the world would be so interested in disgusting bits of twig as to cart them from halfway round the world!"

Stewed apple would never be the same without them. No more clove drops.

"You'll miss her, all the same," I suggested.

Eddie's eyes went red, he drank the hot brew down to its sugary base, managing to hang on to the cloves to spit them into the empty glass. I was full of admiration.

"You don't get two mothers, Pips. Only one."

"Some people would consider that a blessing."

"I do, I do. And yet . . . there's the sadness. For what might have been."

"There's always that, Eddie."

For everything.

"You know, Pips, sometimes I lie awake at night and wonder."

"Is this when there's a full moon, or in the absence of one?"

"That just about sums it up! Every time I bare my soul to you, to get near, you push me away with what everyone calls your wonderful wit."

Eddie could never have a drink and hold his tongue. I dipped my finger in the sugary dregs and licked it.

"Must get back." I smiled to calm the savage breast.

31

However, "back" I was not allowed. We drove as far as the sewage works on Howth Hill and parked the car. In silence, we ate the cheese sandwiches Eddie bought on the seafront. A glass of wine would have cheered them up but this was to be a day of suffering, however hard I tried to escape it. At least my karma would be clocking up.

"I'd like to show you something," Eddie said, though without that gleam in his eye with which he usually prefaced such statements.

I followed him up the narrow track, embedded with sharp Howth stone in green, purple and yellow. .

"That's the Devil's Bit down there." He nodded at the collection of black rocks the sea foamed over. Not the ideal place for a picnic.

"That's where Ophelia used to threaten me with extinction if I didn't carry her wet swimsuit. It still gives me the shivers."

Perhaps that was why Eddie took up archaeology. Dead people are harmless.

At the top of the hill I stopped to look out over the harbour. Mast-to-mast the yachts were at anchor, except for those of the foolish few who had taken the day off work and tried to make the most of the stiff wind.

From a green platform, Eddie disappeared into a thicket of gorse. I followed. On the far side, a roofless cottage leaned against the top of the hill. Doorless and windowless, like an empty skull.

"This was the happy holiday home," Eddie said,

with misery. "The whole summer long, for years, we were closeted together, *sans* electric or running water. Mother hated every minute of it. But Ophelia and I used to stand on those rocks and watch out for ships. First to spot one had to give up half their supper biscuit."

"You had biscuits?"

He ignored me and stared at the cottage.

The outside walls were studded with broken pieces of glass and crockery, green, blue, amber and willow pattern. A child's house, built of scraps. Inside, two tiny rooms and a fireplace in one corner.

"Cosy," I said, smiling at an unusually sad Eddie.

"Too close for comfort! You can imagine what happened when it rained! Feelya and I would sit at this window and count how long it took for a raindrop to get to the bottom. They're slow at first, then they gather speed, join up with another one and, as if they get a fright, whizz to the bottom. Mother would sit in the corner beside the smoking fire, chew aspirin and drink hot milk. Father only came at weekends. Our liberator. He had a little van we climbed into to be carted off to see the world."

"Happy days." I smiled, though perhaps I shouldn't have. I wanted an end to all this reminiscence.

Eddie pulled a briar from its moorings, and I immediately felt a heel.

"Let's go up on the hill and see if there's a boat coming in," I suggested, stretching out a hand. He took it and we made our way up the heather-covered rock.

Ireland's Eye lay still, like a beached whale you could almost touch. Not a sign of a white horse, or a ship. I felt cold and alone. Eddie's misery had touched me more than I wished. I wanted a good book and a warm bed.

"Time I was getting back, Eddie. The nineteenth century is waiting for me."

He gave me that peculiar look again. I could have sworn his bottom lip quivered. But I didn't look too closely.

I put out my hand. Stupidly. He took it, kissed it and held it against his cheek as he shuddered slightly.

"I can't believe I'll never see her again; before, there was always the hope she'd tell me I was OK, that she liked me. But now . . ."

"You must have loved her a lot," I remarked, dislodging a stone with my shoe and scraping the leather in the process.

He cocked his head to one side. "No. I couldn't honestly say that."

I was dumbstruck in the face of such honesty. One good thing about nineteenth-century painting: it keeps your mind on the less important things in life.

At the bottom of the hill a grey-haired woman was bent over a bed of arum lilies, cutting the tallest and cradling them in her arms. Bright orange pistils, like eager lovers with a lot to offer, stared at us.

"The flower of death," Eddie sighed. "Cheer me up some more."

I wanted to yell at him, to tell him to stop wallowing in self-pity, to say that his mother couldn't have lived forever and even if she had would it have made any difference? But I restrained myself with a headache.

"A bit of sea-spray is what we need." I put on my "let's fix this" voice and drove us to the pier. There was the familiar smell of diesel from the boats mixed with the stink of rotting fish behind the warehouses. Probably the ones that were thrown out because of cancerous skins or several eyes and twin tails after a tasty dose of radioactive waste.

We climbed the steps at the end of the pier, being careful to avoid a metal spinning fish with a lethal collection of hooks that an elderly man was attempting to toss into the briny. His fishing kit was like a carpenter's toolbox, with layer upon layer of shelving. Every variety of fly, hook, spinner, lure and gut was arranged in neat compartments.

"Tidier than an artist's paint-box," Eddie said in his "I'm a nice, chatty sort of person" voice.

He got a dirty look for his pains and an even dirtier one when he threw a pebble into the water.

"Fish don't eat stones," he was told.

"They don't eat bits of metal, either." I smiled.

The next cast missed us by a millimetre.

"Not like when we were children," Eddie said, as we left Mr Morose behind. "The old codgers would always let you have a go at flinging out the line or give you a piece of bait and line to fish for crabs."

We climbed into the car.

"Let's get out of here," Eddie said. "That bloody marina has ruined the place."

Chapter Three

❧

I shall be Dean hereafter!

Not one but two surprises waited my return. The first a summons from Professor Goodbody to "Report SAP to my orifice". On official paper, so it wasn't to cook his dinner. The second was a visit from the landlord to tell me he'd decided to marry at the ripe old age of fifty-five. Found someone through the *Farmer's Journal*. He shoved an item outlined in red under my nose. "Well-read, strict TT, pmo. Gertie from Skibbereen. Only one careless owner."

"Terrific sense of humour. Husband carelessly smashed his skull in a head-on." He chuckled. "We've only met twice. But we both knew it at once. First impressions. Can't beat them."

The worst impression in the world, but love is blind, for six months at least.

"My best congrats, Mr Ruddy." I smiled. "Hope she enjoys hoovering."

"Bit difficult from a wheelchair – as a result of the

accident, you see. That's why we need your little abode here. No steps. Unless you'd like the rooms upstairs?"

At an upstairs price, no doubt.

"Perhaps I'll look for a place nearer college. No more waiting for buses in the rain."

"Well, just so long as you're gone by the end of the month. Gertie is giving the place the once-over and measuring for a new bathroom."

She must have had a quick gander at his savings account book as she hugged him to her bosom. Within weeks, the Stannah lift people would be raising her to more distinguished heights.

Professor Goodbody was silhouetted against the wall of his office, his finger halfway up his nose. Breakfast. Just so long as he didn't want to shake hands with me.

"Ah, the wonderful Miss Woodcock." A snotty hand went into his pocket and extricated his half moons. Something about the way his hair fell forward on his head caused me a momentary pang of *je ne sais quoi*. Compassion? Pity? Perhaps he reminded me of my father as he bent towards me in the cot on the one occasion he probably did so. Or perhaps the obstetrician as he extricated my slippery body . . .

"I say, Miss W, did you hear all that?"

I smiled. What can you do when you've been caught napping?

"As I was saying, *two* pieces of good news." He sat on the faded tapestry seat, his large bum dislodging a mushroom cloud of dust mites. "One, Constantia cooks a mean steak and kidney pie – though Matilda would never let kidney into the house, said she could smell the, em, 'piss', as she put it herself. Dear old Bloom loved the 'fine tang', but then so do goats . . . now, where was I?"

God alone knew. "You had a second piece of news?"

"Oh, yes, Woody – I beg your pardon – Miss Woodcock!" He took out a grey handkerchief and mopped his brow. "Though I expect you know your pet name at this stage."

I glared. "Bonkers" was not at all far off the mark – but "Woody"?

"Yes, well, enough of that. Truth is, we had a meeting about it, rather a lengthy one, I may add, though old Corncockle wasn't in the chair, as usual."

I yawned.

"Something about a wonderful discovery in the Boyne Valley, an old pot shard. No! I think it was a piece of linen. Anyway, Corney was all excited about it, took off with a ham sandwich and bottle of Black Bush."

I yawned again. Played with a piece of tissue.

"So, Miss Woody, even with a reduced crew we managed to get through the business. Your name was on the list – all those publications, the long hours you spent burning the midnight oil. Your light is a well-known feature of college life."

It wasn't the time to explain that Eddie couldn't sleep with the light out.

"In fact, there was unanimous agreement about it.

We need a woman in Art History, so, in short, the laurels rest on you, Philippa – if I may be so bold. How does Dean Philippa Woodcock sound?"

One of the few occasions when a feather would have knocked me to *terra firma*.

"Not over the moon, are we? Not that there's any need to lie on the floor and kick your heels in the air; all the same . . ."

What did he want – a kiss? Something worse?

I went into overdrive.

"Absolutely stunned – honoured and delighted. I would be happy to accept – but what exactly does it mean?"

"It means your excellent organisational skills have been recognised, your ability to say nothing when that is the wisest course. Though I must advise a little moderation when it comes to saying what's on your mind. No offence meant – merely a little friendly tip. Henry was our number two choice but he has made a poor showing lately; perhaps he needs time to mellow, like a good claret."

Or perhaps he's a mere Beaujolais, faded after six months.

"So, we're hoping you can organise us. Women are better at that sort of thing, with cricket teas and whist drives behind them."

Thankfully, I'd never done either. I didn't dare ask the important question.

"As for stipend, well, you will be amply rewarded. One of the little perks is free publication."

An extra hundred pounds, in other words, and a hard cover. Better than nothing.

"Of course, the title is everything."

I had to admit "Dean Woodcock" had a certain *éclat*.

Having dispensed with the formalities, Bonkers took a tiny key from where others wear scapulars and opened the cherrywood cabinet in the corner. The doors were inlaid with mother-of-pearl and swung back to reveal Rubens's *Bathers* lit from above to reveal their splendours. He kissed a finger and caressed a large, rounded back. "Ah, Tilly, Tilly," he whispered.

I turned my attention to the heavily-embossed tomes on my left, *The Splendours of Rome* and *Vitruvius Hibernicus*.

He shuffled towards me with a plastic mug full of a blood-red liquid.

"Knock that into you, Woody. Down to your little tippy-toes."

I did my best. In fact, not bad. He brought the bottle and filled us up again.

"All the way from Roundstone where the best sloes are grown."

And the poteen wasn't bad. Goes down a treat.

"You obviously miss Mrs Bonk. . . that is, Mrs Goodbody. Did you manage to get the body back home?"

I didn't know what on earth made me ask such a stupid question.

"Actually, never recovered. Perhaps snagged on

something in the canal or floating around the Med. Strange, not having a body. You keep expecting to meet them in the kitchen slaving over a hot soufflé or floating into harbour at Roundstone. They say everything comes to Roundstone, eventually."

I'm sure they mean Leader grants and retired professors.

"Just a titch for the road." He divided the dregs of bits of skin and twig between us, belched loudly and swallowed without tasting. Such a waste. I sensed a national anthem in the air, so I swilled mine too.

"Before you go, *Lady Dean*," he bowed, "you don't happen to know of a respectable homeless person who would be a type of caretaker to a Georgian mews in Merrion Square?"

Say no more.

❧

Scarcely had I removed my goods and chattels when the squeak of a wheelchair could be heard on the gravel. The landlord's inamorata was wasting no time. Sensible woman. The male of the species is the fickle one; infatuation gives way to indifference. All relationships are the same, in the end.

"Thank you so much, Miss Woodpeck," she said, with a smile that looked as fixed as the laughing policeman. "So nice to get moved in before a Munda morning. Can't abide a Munda. I was just saying to Freddie here, let me lie, for God's sake, of a Munda. Ye see, I'm a divil for the roast beef of a Sunda, d'you know what I mean?"

How to be polite yet not encourage further disclosures is always a torment.

"Well, I won't keep you, you'll want to get settled in," I said, as I raced down the path. There was precious little of her, with two stumps for legs. I was really pleased I'd left the non-slip mat in the bath.

My new abode had a shower and hip-bath combination. Ideal for tea and scones, as you watched the bubbles burst in the happy realisation that you were hidden from public view by a four-storey over basement Georgian house. My mews was an exact replica of a doll's house I'd seen in the *Musée de Chinoiserie* in Paris. The landlady's minder in the main Georgian house confirmed its provenance.

"Dorothea – Dolly to her friends – copied a Ming Dynasty house *exactly*, down to the bamboo furniture." Her set of ill-fitting false teeth clattered at me as she showed me round. "She likes me to look after everything when she's away. South Africa at this time of year. New York in the spring." She dabbed her damp forehead with what looked like a muslin dish-cloth. "No furniture polish, mind. Just a damp cloth and a good airing once a week. No pets and no parties."

Bang goes the poodle I was contemplating. Perhaps a tortoise in the back yard?

"Of course, the little pond in the garden contains fish – be sure to keep the net over it at all times, the seagulls are partial to goldfish. But then they would be, wouldn't they, Miss Woodford."

"Woodcock," I corrected.

"No, we don't approve of keeping birds. Free spirits is what Dolly and me believe in. *Don't fence me in*," she warbled.

Perhaps I ought to think about buying my own house, just me and no one around for miles.

"Beg your pardon, Miss Woodford, I can get quite carried away. Only trying to be friendly. Name's Violet – though I was born in the year of the Tiger."

That would explain the furry chin. The bleached ends caught the light to perfection.

Eventually, Violet entrusted me with the key, warned about baths overflowing on to the imitation William Morris paper and that the bamboo bed was designed for *one*. Suited me. The embrace of a clammy body beneath a hot duvet is not my idea of fun. Postcoital escape is so essential. Visitors would have to slide to the floor.

I scattered my possessions around, put the fridge on and opened a bottle of Lady Langoa. Lying on the couch designed for a midget, I realised that no one knew my whereabouts, no one had my phone number in their little address book. I padded to the French window and stepped on to the patio. On either side the walls were festooned with an intricate network of climbing plants, almost finished shedding their leaves. Beyond, a willow wept across the crazy-paving pathway leading to the little fish-pond whose waters were aerated from the beak of a bronze heron. As soon as they saw my shadow, the fish came to the surface, their mouths open for food like newly-hatched chicks.

"Sorry folks, I've nothing to give," I told them but they wouldn't listen. A bit like people, really. Demanding.

～

Of course, it was Agatha who was the first to track me down.

"Professor Goodbody was amazed you didn't give your only sister your address. He even said you could be a bit of a cold fish at times."

Agatha, in top form.

"Thank you so much for discussing me with the professor. If you want loyalty, don't look for it from your family."

"You've got so uppitty since you got that promotion; God help the world when you get conferred! The rest of us *mere mortals* surely deserve some attention – even if it's only a phone call."

Except Agatha's visits soured whatever piece of pleasure remained when the world had taken its share. But I hadn't the nerve to tell her.

"What do you think of my new abode, anyway?" I asked by way of distraction.

"On the same lines as a little house for entertaining which I designed for a sheik in Saudi, all soft pinks and japonaiserie. Bit old-hat now."

"I won't offer you tea in that case. Not a teabag in the place. Leaves are probably *infra dig* too."

She went to the cocktail cabinet and surveyed the array.

"Don't you think it's a bit early, even for you? Perhaps you'd like to see the fish?"

"I get the distinct feeling I'm not very welcome. I only came to see when you were off to Paris, if that's not classified information too."

"It is. But I'll let you in on the secret: about February – will you miss me?"

She snarled, stretched towards the television buttons and pressed hard. Sisterly love; what did I do to deserve it?

As family, I was obliged to invite Agatha to my "investiture". It took place on a cold morning in mid November, which left a two-inch layer of ice on the fish-pond. A kettle of hot water melted a small hole for the little fellows to breathe and get their din-dins. Cold porridge seemed a cruel thing to give them on such a morning, but then I wasn't privy to the pickings on the bottom of a fish pond. Perhaps it was alive with snails and worms, a veritable palace of piscine pleasure. I carefully drew across the net in case the seagulls were hungry. As I turned, I saw that twitch on the curtains next door. I had sort of noticed it before but decided it was an effect of the wind. There was no mistaking it now. I was being watched. I shivered slightly.

"Sorry, Miss Woodford," Violet, in her woollen dressing-gown, thermal long johns peeping out at the bottom, was on the doorstep. "It's poor Georgie. Had a bad night."

The twitch upon the curtain.

She bent towards me, smelling of sleep and late-night whiskies. "His new, invisible hearing-aid was one side of the lamp and his Moggy the other, but he'd been watching the *African Queen* and all that pulling and heaving the boat tired him out, and between one thing and another – well, he was *certain* it was the Moggy he swallowed, but his cosmetic hearing-aid is gone and the Moggy is still there."

I made a noise to enquire what I could do about it all. I didn't have a metal detector.

"Oh, you needn't worry yourself, Miss Woodford. We'll manage to sort it out. Wouldn't put you out for anything. You've more important fish to fry, you being high up in the University."

I felt exhausted already. And the day had barely begun.

How to carry my ostrich plumes inconspicuously was my first problem. Lady deans were so few and far between that pink ostrich feathers wafting their way out of a black hat were to be the crowning glory of a black silk dress. Where on earth I was to find the money for such finery didn't form part of the list of do's and don'ts for the proceedings. However, Dean Eliza Barratt of Biblical Studies promised to lend me her outfit. After a dry cleaning to remove the stale sweat, and a darn here and there to disguise the moth holes, it was passable. Eddie said I looked *very* fetching.

"But then you'd be gorgeous in sackcloth and ashes," he'd kindly added. I'd really no idea how good-looking I was – but then one never does. I was me, outer and inner. A difficult concept at the best of times.

The Hall was filling up as large black cars disgorged their resplendent contents. *Endimenché* squared. A feather boa tried its damnedest to climb back into the car as its owner wrenched it cruelly into the frosty air.

Eddie, my shadow, stood freezing on the steps. Sometimes I wished he weren't so attentive, so actively proprietorial. A Lady Dean has her pride. She doesn't need a man to lean on. Though perhaps, if she found a real one, she would.

There were hellos everywhere, handshaking and congratulations. I was almost carried away, feeling important, as if I mattered because I'd got a title. Who can spurn adulation, from whatever quarter? However, a "Hi, Pips," from my dear sister soon dispelled any notions I might have been inadvertently harbouring. Not to be outdone, she too had a feather – in front of her hat, where no doubt, *everyone knows* feathers ought to be. The hat was intriguing, like something a ringmaster would wear.

The Chancellor of the college intoned something in Latin. Eddie muttered something under his breath. I felt silly in my pink plumes. Bonkers grabbed my hands.

I let him kiss me, for once, and regretted it when his tongue tried to tickle my tonsils.

"Well, *Dean* Woody!" he said, breathlessly. "We're having a little celebration in your honour. A spot of Madeira and an olive or two in the common room – perhaps a steak and kidney pie later?"

How nice.

"It looks better on you than me," Eliza Barratt whispered as Bonkers was accosted by Henry and Proustina.

"You're being very kind, Eliza. Perhaps if I studied the Bible I'd become as charitable as you are." I smiled.

"Not a bit of it! The most violent tome ever written, beginning with Cain and Abel and ending with a crucifixion! Give me Jane Austen any day. At least people didn't take a hatchet to each other when they disagreed. Look at poor little Fanny Price putting up with that lazy good-for-nothing, Lady Bertram and that unspeakable Aunt Price."

"But that's why poor little Fanny isn't too popular. Most readers feel she was too much of a goody-goody."

"I don't know. There's a lot to be said for restraint, all the same," she said wistfully. Was Dean Barratt holding back on something? Sex? Violence?

We made our way to the common room, declined the Madeira and opted for a gin and tonic. We choose the least lumpy of the couches that held up the walls.

"Philippa," Eliza began in a tone that put me on my guard, "if you don't mind me saying so. . ." She sipped at her drink and wiped her delicate mouth with a georgette handkerchief in pale·violet.

Of course I minded but, like a real trooper, I didn't let it show.

"You don't seem very, what shall I say, thrilled about becoming Dean of Art History."

My look said "Is that so?" so she battled on.

"I remember when I got a belt of the Chancellor's staff I was over the moon. At last I'd made it. My father always said I should aim for nothing lower, and Pappy was right, as usual."

She waved for a second G and T. I declined, wondering how I could make a graceful escape before childhood traumas reared their heads.

"Well, I suppose I am pleased at my 'honour'," I rushed in to take her mind off herself. "I haven't figured out just what it means yet, except for the fancy stationery and a larger office."

"Power is what it means, Philippa, power. You can now lord it over the whole motley crew. Whip them into submission. Make them eat dirt."

I could smell the brimstone, see the coals of hellfire glowing.

"Doubt if I'd have the time for all that, Eliza." I surreptitiously disgorged the olive stone into my palm. "I'm too busy a mortal to have any energy left to wield that sort of power. Besides, half the fun is when someone fights back."

"Let them do that and you're sunk, Philippa. They'll drag *you* down. Make no mistake. Deans are there to be attacked. Part of the establishment. It's you or them, Philippa."

Perhaps I should have paid more attention to her words. We only do what we can.

After my third G and T I sank back into the horse-hair and let my normally controlled brain have a little holiday. Proustina and Henry were *tête-à-tête* beneath a copy of Dürer's *Adam & Eve*, sharing some intimacy, she flashing teeth, he eyes and mouth agog. The twins were in definite danger, and only three years old.

"About that steak and kidney pie, Philly." Bonkers, eyes glazed, mouth moist with hope.

"Have to take a raincheck, Prof. Date with a vegetable stew, I'm afraid."

My night for macrobiotic cooking.

"Always said you were a rock of sense. Never the last to leave a party," Eliza Barrett sounded almost envious.

"You just get up and go, Eliza," I said.

"The hardest thing of all with free G and T." She waved me goodbye.

Not when you consider the cost of a new liver.

I made a detour past Henry. "How are little Sue and Prue?" I enquired. "Bet they're growing apace," I rubbed salt.

He had the grace to blush. Proustina blinded me with her teeth. Strange how she didn't get bits of tea leaf or peanut stuck between them like the rest of us. Probably the Teflon coating.

Bonkers made another dive for me as I woozled my

way out the door. His hand on my left bicep just happened to stray across my breast. Then all hell broke loose. My hand unfortunately knocked his glass for seven and, being unbalanced, I accidentally stamped on his toe. Just as well he was slightly anaesthetised.

Suddenly, there was a crash inside the room. I peered through the door. Agatha, on the floor like a fallen clothes-stand. Feather and hat very bent. Glass still in her hand.

In seconds I was beside her, trying to find a pulse and failing. Her white face had a tinge of green. I slapped it. Rubbed her cheeks. Tried to lift her.

"I'll call an ambulance." Eddie.

People were closing in. Not half as daft as he appeared, Bonkers was pushing back the crowd, ushering them out of the room.

"How unfortunate!" Proustina slobbered a bibful, as usual.

I got Ag's head on to a cushion. An eyelash flickered. Not dead yet. I slapped a bit more. With difficulty, managed to prise the glass from her hand. Someone brought a blanket. I removed her shoes and rubbed her feet, stone cold in her white tights. A rag doll without its stuffing.

"Don't get upset, Pips," Eddie said gently, an arm round my shoulders.

I wiped the snot from my lip and rubbed my eyes on my sleeve.

"Looks like she hadn't had breakfast. Too much gin on an empty stomach," Eddie said. "But she'll be OK."

I didn't believe him.

"It's my fault. I should have been nicer to her, offered her breakfast before the ceremony."

"Was it you who held the glass and poured the gin down her neck?"

"No. But all the same . . ."

Except for the locked doors, no one would have guessed we were in the loony bin. And the bronze bust of St Loman.

"If you'd wait twenty minutes, she should be awake then."

The detox unit were trying to flush the alcohol from Ag's bloodstream.

"How long has she been drinking so heavily?"

I looked at Eddie, bewildered. How long indeed?

"I'm afraid I've no idea. Had no idea she was, to *that* extent."

She pursed her lips.

"Not unusual for the family to be the last to know."

Agatha was groggy but alive. I smiled in gratitude.

"God, I could murder a gin and tonic," she slurred.

"That's exactly what will murder *you* if you don't give it up."

She turned her back and within seconds was snoring.

Eddie put an arm round me and led me quietly from the room. If I hadn't been crying so much, I would have screamed my head off.

As I pulled the curtains on the dark night I saw something move in the garden. I turned out the light. Two shapes. Violet and the window watcher, if I wasn't mistaken. Violet turned and waved. Didn't miss a trick.

I joined them.

"Hope you don't mind, Miss Woodfern. To spare the oilyfactories, poor Georgie's brought his bucket outside to look for that expensive hearing-aid," she whispered.

She needn't have bothered whispering, since George was deaf as a post. His brow dripping sweat, he held a metal detector over a bright yellow bucket. The obvious began to dawn.

"You don't get the stink if you stand downwind." Vi giggled.

"What happens if he gets, sort of, you know – constipated?"

"Just takes longer, I suppose. Or it gets lodged in the cracks and fissures."

I could have enumerated a thousand possibilities but I restrained myself. Purgatorial at times.

"Well, the doctor did offer to put him in touch with one of those clinics that hose you out, if you'll pardon me."

"Perhaps something less drastic, like a macrobiotic diet, would do the trick."

"No. Antibiotics don't agree with him. 'Jangly insides' he says he has, from his mother. A third cousin once removed of the Guinness's. Poor dear had to take *a lot* of stout to cure the janglies."

I knew the feeling.

Suddenly, a squeal from the dark shape guddling in the bucket. He turned. Between a very brown thumb and forefinger, he held aloft a piece of metal.

"Good on ye!" Violet screeched.

I turned for home. Supper was inconceivable. *The Tibetan Book of Living and Dying* anchored me to the one important thing in life. Death. Brown fingers seemed tame in comparison.

Chapter Four

❧

I at length to merry Paris came

Paris in winter is scoured clean by a biting wind. It caused tears to trickle and petrify on my cheekbones.

"Mong Dew," Mary said in her Dublin French. "You've a drip on the end of your nose that'd drown a cat. Here, give a quick wipe." She handed me a towel. "I've been telling Lord and Lady Muck inside that they're expecting a dean. That snot would make them think you were a normal person."

I supposed Mary thought she was a normal too. My lips were frozen together, so I did what I was told.

The heat from the apartment hit me like hot air under a car bonnet, including the smells. Oil, definitely. Madame was pandering to foreign tastes and serving chips.

"She fancies herself as Paris's answer to Madhur Jaffrey. Afraid it's samosas, parath nan and curry." She jerked a thumb towards a half-closed door from which thin wisps of smoke were curling towards the cold air in the hallway. "But don't worry. They've a dog who's a girl's best friend sitting under the table."

A large bulk came towards us from the end of a narrow corridor.

"Monsieur Lagoute, *Dean* Woodcock," Mary said with due reverence. I played the game and inclined my head gracefully. Anything for a free meal.

Monsieur lifted my cold hand and feathered it with his thin lips. Slight something there; perhaps he was merely hungry.

"*Enchanté*, Madame Dean," he inclined his head towards me. It sat on top of his shoulders without visible means of support. Napoleonic. He even held his left breast with his right hand as he ushered me into a tiny sitting-room.

I *did* like the cocktail cabinet. Deeply carved and sloping to one side in true pre-Louis XV fashion, it stretched back for several feet in layer, upon layer of various concoctions. I decided on the Pinot de Charenton. Pure nectar when it's good. And Monsieur looked as if he knew his Pinot.

Madame still hadn't appeared as Nappy poured another libation. Mary was obsequiously grateful. Obviously not used to being so well treated.

"You are an art historian," Monsieur confirmed for me. "Excuse me, but what does that involve?" he asked.

I blinded him with facts, figures, styles and schools. He yawned after two minutes, stuck an enormous cigar between his teeth and embraced it with his lips. Slightly unsubtle, I felt. Notwithstanding, I soldiered on, pondering aloud the influences of a David, the drama of an Ingrès. Not until Madame appeared, reeking of Yves St Laurent and boiling oil, did I draw breath.

She made a beeline for me. I held out my glass. "Really good Pinot," I remarked. However, she ignored my glass and compliment, came even closer, sort of stumbled into my arms and pulled at my hair.

"For Chrissake, Philippa, she's trying to kiss you!" Mary said in English.

Now that I knew what was happening, I managed to help Madame regain a little balance, untangle her bracelet from my hair and proffered a warm cheek. Though I'd really have preferred another Pinot.

Dinner was the usual French business of making *grande chose* out of precious little. For starters there were squares of streaky bacon, simmered till the fat melted, when chunks of potatoes were piled in to cook in the juice. Quite delicious. Monsieur offered a harmless little wine made on the cousin's *propriété*. It didn't quite go with the bacon, but after a few mouthfuls – who cared?

Nappy was into farm machinery in a big way, he told us, as Madame cleared the table for the entrée. "We sell all over the world – except in Irlande, the market is too small."

Mary and I bridled at this and were about to protest

when the door opened. A small, quite beautiful child with long, black pigtails came into the room.

"Maman, I saw him again. The ghost!"

Monsieur sniggered and tucked into dinner. Curry. Mouth-blisteringly hot. A dish that should be left where it belonged – in hot countries, to drown the taste of rotting meat.

"What did the ghost say to you this time?"

"He said for me to tell Papa he had left his car lights on."

Dead silence. We all looked at Papa. Sweat had broken out on his forehead and the tip of his nose. He swallowed a pint of Vittel.

"Nonsense," he said, mopping his brow and collapsing into his chair. "Go back to bed at once."

"Perhaps, just to make sure, you would have a look?" Madame appealed.

He threw his napkin on to the table, pulled a cigar from his pocket and stuck it between his lips.

"A real charmer there," I said to Mary in English.

"He's lost face in front of not only women but *foreign* women."

How awful.

Madame served the dessert.

"A favourite of my mother. Baked almonds with fresh cheese."

Sounded peculiar but it was light, nutty and creamy.

Monsieur returned, sullen, to the table and refused pudding, just to get his face back. He clipped his cigar, lit and blew its noxious fumes at us. He looked almost his old self again.

"The child was quite right. She must have seen them from the window."

Mary raised a disbelieving eye and Madame kept her head down. Nappy obviously always got the last word.

After the coffee and *petit fours*, Monsieur and Madame retired to the lounge while Mary and I lingered over the last of the wine and a bowlful of cherries.

"Napoleon seems decidedly cantankerous," I remarked.

"He's OK, really." Poor Mary tried to make the best of it. "Has to have physiotherapy three times a week. Some sort of circulation problem."

"I thought there was something. No blood getting to his brain."

"Still the same old Pips! I've missed your jaundiced view of humanity. So often I think, my God, what's wrong with *me*? When in fact it's other people. They're unbelievable at times. At least Monsieur spares me his hot, clammy breath where it's not wanted! The last one seemed to be in a permanent state of tumescence, unlike gorillas who need to have a presenting female nearby."

"Perhaps his non-return valve got stuck."

"Whatever it was, I was stuck with him! Madame held her head up, eyes fixed on the middle distance, pretended everything was totally normal. But that bulge was unmistakable. I was really tempted to enter a convent. Even sent for the brochures but the Mère Superieur reminded me of my mother, so that was that. In the end, I just left after being chased up and down the marble stairs for hours one evening while Madame attended her clairvoyant. I'm learning to hate men."

I felt she was coming to that a little late but said nothing. Better late than never. Though I did feel it incumbent upon me to cheer her up a little.

"Never mind, Mary. As soon as someone you actually like hoves into harbour, you'll cast your scruples to the wind."

"That'd be just like it," she said, disgusted.

We sipped our cognac in silence.

I'd timed my arrival to coincide with a Siberian wind that raged for a week. Not even thermal silk long johns kept the cold at bay, though the feel of silk against one's skin is heavenly, like the flesh of a lover – so they say. I spent my time watching French television with Mary, drinking the Lagoutes' Pinot and, when the headaches got too much, we moved on to the very passable Chablis. We ate baguettes laced with crisps and ham. Madame insisted on cooking supper when she returned from her boutique which sold lacy underwear, some of which she promised me. Mary had more than she would wear in a lifetime.

However, by the middle of the second week, I panicked and told Mary I'd have to do some work or I would be the shortest-serving dean in history. So I took the métro to Sacré Coeur and walked the rest of the way to Montmartre, the most touristy destination of them all, but the one that never ceases to entertain. Only one or two artists were out of their bed, copying dreamy-looking women from black and white photographs to drum up custom for their portraits. I skipped into *La Tasse de Thé*, the tourist grabber. Real tea, black as treacle, was promised. I settled for a *café crème* and brioche, fresh from the oven – no bowing to modernity with microwaves. *Le patron* had the jaded air of a man who had seen too many fleeting faces and too much poor wine, neither doing much good for body or spirit. I smiled. Wonder of wonders, he smiled back.

"How long?" he asked of my visit.

"Forever," I replied.

He laughed, poured himself a *petit café*, squirted a measure of cognac into it and said *Salut*. He swallowed the lot and poured another.

"Time was when La Butte was really something," he said, sucking on a Gauloise. "Then, you knew everyone. It was 'Vincent' or 'Toulouse'. All gone now."

I didn't like to interrupt his reverie to remind him that that was almost a century ago and he didn't seem a day over sixty. Relief came in the form of a red-haired, none too tall, person of the opposite sex. The *patron* barely lifted his head from the dish of freshly-made pâté and bottle of red wine he was about to open. "The *Deuxième Cru* are underrated, you know," he said, sniffing the cork.

"Sounds just like my mother," an American drawl

poured from the redhead. "'Jack, she says, you will never be first class but try to be a darn good second class, willya?'"

"Ah, Monsieur O'Connor!" *Le patron* exclaimed, a little too reverently for my liking. One should be circumspect with Americans. There is a fine line between friendship and familiarity.

They embraced *à la Bretonne*, kissing on each cheek and again on the first, just to be sure. I averted my eyes, casting them around the Gauloise-stained walls, covered with photographs of *artistes* being hugged by *Le Patron*. High up, in a corner, was a portrait of a young child with big round eyes and an armful of flowers. There was something about the mouth that was familiar.

"Marlene," *Le patron* informed, as he and Mr O'Connor came to sit with me. "In better days," he added.

A fresh coffee, unasked for, therefore free. I decided to be on my best behaviour.

"My grandfather was Irish." Mr O'Connor smiled. Not a bad set of teeth.

"We're everywhere, like weed seeds," I replied.

He dropped his eyelid for a second, gathered a little courage and said: "A little derogatory?"

"*Au contraire*, a weed is merely a flower out of place." I sipped my coffee.

"You seem to be a bit of a thistle!" He slapped his sides and let out a laugh that would shatter glass. *Le Patron*'s tummy shook like a mound of wriggling puppies.

Great fun!

"It's nearly lunch. How about a bite to eat?" my colonial acquaintance asked.

"I've quite a bit of work to do – in the Gallery. I've to put six months work into less than three weeks."

"I'll escort you there. Make sure you're not, eh . . . *waylaid*."

"I'm prepared for anything." I showed him my umbrella, one specially fortified with pieces of lead. Murder to carry but so comforting.

We got up to go. The *patron* stared at us thoughtfully, gathered the empty cups and disappeared behind a beaded curtain.

"*Au revoir*," we shouted to the rattling curtain but got no reply.

In the harsh winter sun outside, Jack O'Connor had the sort of rough skin you often see in Dublin's inner city, an underglaze of white with a red wash. He seemed to have been vaccinated with a gramophone needle, had told me his life history by the time we'd left La Butte far behind.

"Doing research on my father," he said, planting an empty pipe in his mouth.

American mothers tend to wean too early, leave the little dears gasping for oral satisfaction, doomed to chew gum or suck a pipe.

"I've discovered Pop spent some time here during the war. What doing, I don't know. He left some papers with a friend. Long since dead of course, but she left a huge pile of stuff with her daughter, Sophie, who's *very* much alive and well."

I detected a slight ripple of affection.

"So, Sophie's allowed me to rummage through all these papers. Gosh, what a job! You've got to number them all and list them, otherwise you're in deep do-do. However, I've learned a great deal."

I was dying to know just the interesting details, but forbore to enquire.

"Seeing you're not gonna ask, I'll tell you." He sucked on his empty pipe for an eternity. The noise of spittle being dragged through a small hole was as uplifting as fingernails scraping across a worn blackboard.

"God, I must get rid of this thing," he said, knocking the pipe off a lamppost.

Amen to that.

"Looks like I've a whole 'other' family I knew nothing about in gay Paree. At least three – a boy and two girls. Red-haired, which shouldn't be difficult to find. Trouble is, you can't really go up to someone and ask if their father was a randy Irishman, now can you?"

I merely stared back. The question could have applied to thousands.

"Well, I couldn't, Yank and all that I am."

Mercifully he put the pipe into his pocket, followed it with his hands.

We parted at the Louvre after more coffee and pipe-sucking. I'd an hour to spare before they shut. I needn't have bothered. I looked at the pictures but all I could see was Jack O'Connor's red hair and face, smell his pipe – my clothes seemed impregnated with St Bruno – and hear again every word we spoke. I decided I was *dépaysé* and Jack was merely a friendly voice.

Fool that I was.

He was at the gallery before me the following morning, his hair carefully combed and gelled. He reminded me of a lily on a cold day, pristine but distant.

We stood together, but I couldn't think of a thing to say.

"Cold weather we're having for the time of year," Jack said stiffly. "Well, you Irish are always talking about the weather. Just wanted to make you feel at home."

"That's because we *have* something to talk about. We can get snow in July, you know, or sandstorms from the Sahara. Our skies are full of drama."

"Just like the women."

I treated that like a bird dropping and left it where it fell.

"Anyway, Philippa old trout, how's about that bite to eat? Pick you up about noon, if you're amenable."

I gave him my very best smile and went through the glass doors.

No sooner had I got my notebook and my list of pictures out than I went into a daze. I reminded myself of how much my time-wasting was costing me, that it was silly agreeing to lunch – I should have said dinner, then I'd have a full day of concentration. What did I see in this fellow anyway? After an hour's deliberation and two cups of coffee, the best I came up with was that he either intrigued me or I was bored and welcomed any diversion.

True to his word he was waiting outside the doors, a small package in his hand.

"A book I thought you'd enjoy," he said.

Marguerite Duras *L'Amant*.

"It was the most dog-eared book at school. All the *important* pages were dog-eared, underlined and translated."

"Here, I'll take it back. Get you something else." Jack tried to grab it from me.

"No! I mean, don't bother. It's a present."

I put the book into my folder and talked about the weather.

From the outside, the restaurant looked nondescript, slightly unkempt, even. But they had *pommes de terre*, so I acquiesced.

Once inside, my impression soared. A roaring log fire. The unmistakable scent of apple-smoke. I remembered Nellie's little cabin home in Dunquin, looking out towards the Blaskets where she'd been born.

"My, we're silent."

"Marcel was right. The sense of smell is the strongest of them all."

"Don't tell me, it's the fire, right?"

I nodded.

"Apple? Crab, Bramley or, heaven forfend, Golden Delicious?"

An answer caught in my throat. I was putty in the hands of anyone who knew about "nature".

"You're holding my hand," I said stupidly.

"It's a bit naughtier than that, Philippa. I'm *touching* you."

For the second time in my life, I blushed.

I didn't know whether it was the heat, the wine – a bottle of Chateauneuf du Pape with the wild boar *and* a bottle of Barsac for the pud – the red hair and smiling eyes, or the sharp wit and oceans of poetry he was able to quote word-perfect that did it; what was certain was that, as he helped me into my Afgan coat and whispered an invitation to go back to his hotel, I said yes. Or "OK", to be exact.

I hadn't of course realised it wasn't too far away, or was it a case of wishing it were? Anyway, we were there in next to no time, past the ageing concierge who, like more French people than the national statistics would care to be aware of, had one eye looking east and the other west. Which was fine today. We went up.

And up. One of those cheap hotels, cheap because they've no lift. Built tall and skinny, there wasn't a scrap of space left to install a lift, unless the bedrooms were to be halved. And James, or Jack, as I was to call him, was installed on the top floor, the cheapest room of all. Only for the young. The arthritic kept to *terra firma*.

We stopped several times to catch our breath, but lost it again kissing each other like mad, even drawing blood on at least one occasion. Mr O'Connor boded well.

Yet how crazy! A complete stranger. Though as Nellie, who looked after me as a child, always said, "Sure, you can't go far wrong with an Irishman". "Far" being the operative word. On the third floor, I feared for my life and wondered how I could escape quickly down the twisting, ankle-breaking stairs. Such is romance, it perishes on the rock of reality.

At that point I almost went cold.

"OK, Philippa?" My companion looked deeply into my eyes. I had difficulty focusing on his. Even his voice seemed to come down a tunnel.

"It's the altitude sickness," he said, deadpan. And then laughed his head off.

I knew then I'd be OK. Anyone who enjoyed life as much as he did had no need to inflict injury on someone else.

He had my coat hanging up, a glass of port in one hand and a teeny-weeny joint between my fingers in next to no time. Not since I was a headless student had I been so reckless.

He filled his pipe with tobacco shreds from a plastic bag and from a tiny wooden box took a pinch of the same weed, layering it like a *salade composée*.

We lit up. And within seconds, a glow settled on the world. It was amazing I hadn't noticed how beautiful the room was; in fact, it was the nicest room

I'd ever been in, the best-sprung chair I'd ever made contact with. And Jack – well, he was just about the greatest thing I'd ever known. He was my ideal, the one I'd been searching for, the one I'd never felt so strongly about, the one I could see me spending lots and lots of time with, the one I'd never tire of, who would constantly amuse, entertain, instruct. But was he any good in bed?

That feeling got stronger and stronger.

"I think I need a bit of air," I suggested, playing for time.

Jack got up from the floor, where he'd been telling me his thoughts on the Ming Dynasty and feeding the tiny grate with pieces of smokeless fuel.

"Maybe you ought to lie down."

Being prone, on cool, clean damask sheets was heavenly. Fire still raged but my control tower told it to cool down, keep my clothes on, it was still winter.

However, control sensibly looks the other way when it comes to matters of the flesh. Just as well. Otherwise the earth would bear nothing but trees.

"You sure about this?" Jack asked.

I said nothing. Just moved slightly. It was enough.

"Don't you ever do that again!" Mary hissed, curlers still in place, as she quietly closed the door. "Didn't get a wink of sleep worrying about you. Thought you were soup in some *pied-noir*'s cauldron."

I repeated my apologies. I hadn't, for even an instant, stopped to consider the possibility that she'd be waiting and worrying – or indeed, anything else. Too late now. From the time I'd discarded my laddered tights, pulled on my skirt and left the sleeping Mr. O'Connor, I'd mentally whipped myself a dozen times. To the worry of AIDS, crabs, and whatever delicacy was lurking in Mr O'Connor's nether regions, I'd added some of my own: being intimate with someone I'd known less than forty-eight hours, pregnancy and the worst hangover I'd ever experienced.

"The pot was probably cheap, rotten stuff off the Algerian banana boats."

So, my brain could explode at any moment. Served me right.

"Anyway, what was he like?"

"Obviously out to take advantage," I heard myself lie.

"Did you put up a bit of a fight, though?" Mary asked, concerned.

"Not the slightest. That's what I'm so disgusted about. Me, who wouldn't dream of lying next to someone unless they produced a health certificate, and had a shower five minutes prior to clambering all over me. You don't happen to have a shotgun handy?"

"I'd have been only too happy to use one on you an hour ago, but seeing as how you're so miserable, I don't feel the urge any more."

"You always were a pal, Mary. Merciful. I remember the spiders you used to save from going down the plughole."

We smiled. Friends again.

My bath took a full hour, by the time I'd scrubbed every pore and crevice I could find. Mary kindly did my back.

Again, I racked my brain. Why on earth had I been so crazy?

Feeling slightly more human, I made my way to the Louvre to do the work I came to do in the first place. Fortunately the rush hour was over, so I got to walk on the pavement. Paris was fast becoming like Tokyo, not a square inch of space to spare.

I made straight for the coffee shop to take a swig of the potion I'd met as a schoolgirl on my first French trip. Bright yellow and tasting vile, *Schoum* numbs the innards like nothing else. Followed by two coffees, I felt almost normal enough to take a look at my notes: today the Ingrès and David were earmarked for examination. It's always better to stand before a painting, write the first words that come into your head when looking at it, and *then* read all the books about it. The similarities and comparisons are often surprising.

"Not the most heartfelt goodbye I've ever had!"

Jack O'Connor, of all people. I felt my mouth open but nothing come out.

Stupidly I felt tears rush forth, while words failed me.

"God, Philippa, I didn't mean to sound so angry." He sat beside me and took my hand. I felt strangely shy. And comforted.

He lifted my chin, gently. His eyes were the bluest blue I'd ever seen in the light of day. They had laughter at their bottom, not sadness like the ones I see in the mirror.

"Really enjoyed . . . no, that doesn't sound too, em . . . what I'd like to say is . . . well, I never felt so . . . maybe you like the smell of these?"

He produced a thick bunch of short-stemmed freesias from his briefcase.

"I always thought it was sandwiches men carried in those things," I said, in case I went hysterical with gratitude and wonder and something else I wasn't quite sure of. "Yes, I love their perfume. Poignant. Evocative."

"I just love your big words, Philippa. I think, y'know, I just love you."

Honesty is the curse of love. We can hide behind games. I sniffed at my bouquet and said nothing. Those smiling blue eyes, that curved mouth . . .

"Better get on and do some work," I said, brushing off invisible crumbs.

"Perhaps, if you'd like, Philippa, we could meet in a couple hours, have a quick bite to eat and take a look at those papers of my dad's, as you promised – last night."

So long as that was all I promised.

"Well, I can hardly go back on my word, Jack." One last outing and that would be that. Pity. Fortunately I hadn't told him I was a *dean*. It would give academia an even worse name than it has already.

Naked men in the Davids, Delacroixs and Ingrès were

most provoking and a distraction to serious study. Their muscled legs and shoulders seemed made for quieter pursuits than war, their bloodied bodies a hymn to death and glory.

I met Jack in the foyer; the few scribbles and sketches in my pocket the meagre result of two hours work.

"How'd it go?" he asked.

"It didn't. Too much blood and death. No wonder the Impressionists were popular. All that joy after so much darkness."

He held my hand. Very comforting, in the circumstances. Even I had to admit it. Sometimes it's almost pleasant not to be alone.

"Ruined your appetite?"

I refused to answer that one.

One good thing about Paris in winter is the cafés are almost empty and the waitresses almost pleased to see you – though a really happy one is as scarce as hens' teeth.

"*Déculottes tes pensées,*" Jack said in that very American way of his that cut right to basics.

"I was contemplating happiness, that's all." I smiled that that was the end of the matter.

"My favourite yarn about happiness is the one where Mrs de Gaulle was asked by a journalist what she most valued in life. She said, 'Ah . . . pinus', at which the General almost keeled over in consternation. 'Chérie,' he whispered, 'zee word is '*appiness.*'"

He gave his glass-shattering laugh.

I looked at the menu, and breathed.

The dishes that arrived, hot and extremely edible, were despatched effortlessly. Except for the pudding, which we shared with a bottle of passable Sauternes. The best I ever had was in a rooftop restaurant at La Boule when I was about fifteen. But I was a growing girl then. My capacity isn't what it was. So, I allowed Jack the last glass.

"Cheers, Pippy. Really enjoying your company."

Why do people have to spoil everything by *expressing* the obvious?

"The food is good, too. And the wine."

Especially the *digestif* – Tia Maria, with cream.

"'Spose we'd better get some of these papers of Pop's done, before *we're* done." His laughter caused the lights to flicker and the waitresses to reach for the anti-choking tongs.

More in control of myself than yesterday, and only slightly wobbly, I negotiated the winding staircase, managing to allow two residents to pass without serious mishap, but a third caught her hatpin in my coat and accused me of trying to steal it. Jack calmed her down and her toothless smile was finally restored.

"Just coffee for me," I stated as soon as we were seated before a table piled high with yellowing papers and battered cardboard boxes.

"Of course. What else?"

I didn't react. The room reverberated with that dreadful laughter again. My stay/go buttons went on red alert and then got stuck somewhere in the middle.

"Sorry, Pips. I was just remembering the pleasure you took in that little, em, trip you had yesterday."

"Thank you for reminding me!"

My hand was lifted to that soft, curved mouth, kissed and caressed. Whatever about "little trips", certainly not the feathers again!

I recited lines from *Tintern Abbey* to steady myself, as my hand underwent the most blatant massage with a pointed, pink tongue. However, "The nurse, the guide, the guardian and soul of all my moral being" soon melted like snow as the tongue continued its voyage of discovery. I called on all those images taught me on my mother's lap, designed to make a girl pull back from the brink – mother's disapproving face, father's disapproving face; Nellie's total incomprehension, and the bottom of the barrel: smelly STs. But that glow came back again, the one that gets a girl in its grip and promises pleasure.

"Really sorry, Philippa." With resources that I seemed bereft of, he pulled away from me and grabbed a bunch of papers. "You'll think me a dreadful rake, inveigling you here day after day to have my wicked way with you."

That is, at least partly, what the male and female thing is about. Otherwise, we'd spend our time with a goldfish.

However, after an hour poring over papers, making notes, sorting and filing I was ready for a little pick-me-up.

"I'll put the kettle on," Jack said, placing a hand on my shoulder as he went past into the kitchen. I followed to lend a hand and get the blood moving in my veins. Attic rooms are iceboxes.

"Y'know," he said, "I think my Dad was a class of spy. For the Americans. Either that or he was in the pay of the Mafia."

I enquired about the evidence leading up to this conjecture.

"The money. Where on earth did he get the quantities of dollars it must have taken to keep two families, two wives and a lover?"

"Not on the dole, anyway," I remarked.

That laugh once more.

"You're really dry, Philippa! Really . . . *earthy*."

We were close together over the coffee cups and teaspoons. He looked that look, the one that feels like hell – dissatisfaction, longing, plain old animal desire. I didn't budge an inch. No encouragement this time. But as he leant towards me, I knew I wouldn't turn away; couldn't turn away.

Today, the sheets were pale blue with yellow stars, or perhaps my head was just spinning. I couldn't blame the wine, the weed or the *digestif*. It could hardly be love – after three days! Though a lifetime of knowing someone doesn't guarantee affection. It was just stupidity probably, sheer idiocy.

"This has never happened to me before, Philippa. I've never been so intimate with someone, so soon . . ."

"Are you trying to say it's all *my* fault, leading *you* astray?" I prepared to get up from the crushed sheets.

And was firmly pulled amongst them again. And again.

When a navy blue sky appeared outside the tiny attic window, Jack put on Percy Sledge's ontological scream, *When a Man Loves a Woman*. I tried to pull myself into some semblance of normality. Once is forgivable. Twice seemed a bit of a habit.

"Hear that, Philippa! When a man falls in love with a woman he can't keep his mind 'on nothing else, he'd trade the whole world for the good thing he sees'."

"Don't look at me like that," I warned. "It's up to you where you place your affections. Don't blame me!"

"But it *is* you, Philippa! It's not the receptionist downstairs, or the skinny little lady whom you tried to *dérobe* of her cute little hatpin!"

"It simply got caught . . ." And then I saw the grin, and watched the bubbles that started in his toes and erupted in a shower above his head. "That laugh will get you into serious trouble one of these days," I warned, as I pulled on my coat and grabbed my empty notebook.

"Going so soon? The night's but a pup!"

"The knight *is* a pup. My guilty conscience might just spur me into doing some work, thank you just the same."

He helped me button my coat and put on my gloves.

"I was going to pop something into the microwave

and then I thought maybe we'd do the Paris thing – the clubs on the Boulevard St Germain, maybe a coffee in *Les Deux Magots*. Who knows who we might run into there. I hear Anita Brookner is in town and Paul Theroux . . ."

"Well, perhaps if I got up late – I mean early – in the morning I could write about Van Gogh's Dutch period. Maybe Manet's social realism. Yes, that sounds sensible, instead of trying to flog myself. Totally inimical to good work."

"I couldn't agree more," he said, as he unbuttoned my coat and a few other items and brought me several edible delicacies on a tray amongst the blue sheets with yellow stars.

The hot, sweet air almost drove us back from the pulsating throng in *À Milo*. Thick slabs of hash lay on the counter like chunks of cheese.

Several joints in a row and you're hooked into an expensive and time-consuming habit. Life is too short to waste it living in the extremes of heaven or absolute hell. I decided on cognac.

"Guess you're right, Philippa. We have each other, after all."

I must be slipping. He was obviously feeling more confidence than was healthy. Love thrives on uncertainty.

I phoned Mary to tell her I might be late.

"Again? Who *is* this guy? You've been here less than ten days and already hitched up with someone with the stamina of Casanova! Can I find someone, too? How do you go about it?"

I could have advised her to act as insanely as me but my pride got in the way. I left the silence in the air say whatever she wanted to hear.

"Charm, obviously, Philly. I'm too direct. Not mysterious enough. Whereas you – you always manage to keep something in reserve. I bet it's your sense of humour. I'm far too serious. I want to believe it will be forever."

"Life is not forever, Mary. One never knows whether the sun will rise tomorrow. A dicky nuclear reactor could go off in the night and fry us in our beds."

"Charming! I just love the smell of burnt meat."

I returned to the fray, now hotter and even more frantic. A trio of well-endowed females were busy disporting themselves under the dazzling lights, removing unwanted clothes to the delight of the onlookers. Jack sat in a shaft of red light that gathered like a halo about his head. Seeing me, he smiled that smile. I knew then I was doomed, doomed to find my happiness depended on someone else, for this was love.

"Got us a bottle of wine that cost more than a trip on the QE2. The hash is cheaper," he said.

"But a lot more expensive in the long run." I held out my glass. A red Cahors, heavy and earthy, meant for roast beef and a snooze by the fire.

"I hear you thinking heavily there, Philippa."

"Just feeling slightly homesick. For the life I *want* to live. It's totally out of reach, impossible."

"Let's cheer you up, dance the blues away."

Like ivy, we clung against each other and made small, animal movements around the dance floor. Nothing like the thrill of body contact when its sequel would be too public to contemplate. Agony and ecstasy. I felt myself being watched and looked at Jack to see if he'd noticed. But he was swooning away, his eyes firmly closed and tiny beads of sweat breaking out on his eyelids. I could see all this because I was at least a foot taller than Jack. His head lay against my collar bone. Not a great fit, except that it didn't seem to matter. Much.

Finally, the dark eyes boring into me became too much.

"Is it my paranoia or is that black person watching me – or perhaps it's you he's ogling!"

Jack squinted. "Black, white polo neck, long thin cigar, black leather boots."

The very one. We sat down. A grave mistake. A person fitting the same description came towards us, waving the long, thin cigar.

"Mademoiselle, may I have the honour?" he asked in an Academie Française accent. I looked at Jack. A shrug. This one was on me. I looked at Mr Black Person. Beyond the *odeur de cigar* I was drawn to a distinct whiff of expensive clothes and hot showers. It was obviously time to leave.

The coffee and *pâtisserie* in *Les Deux Magots* seemed without magic, ordinary. It could have been Bewley's. The collection of beautiful women with their price per hour printed on the sole of their shoe brought me to rock bottom. The deep, black water of the Seine looked inviting. Though I looked deeply into it, I knew I would never take the plunge. However bad life may seem, death is a dead end.

"Anything else cheer you up? Visit to Sophie?" he asked, looking at his watch. "She wouldn't be in bed yet. Likes to hear the World Service."

We heard it on the landing, loud and positive as only the World Service can be. Sophie took a while to reach the door; Jack took advantage of the wait to massage my lips with his. Looking at him in the cold light of the shadeless bulb I saw a man of fifty, still young, though ageing. I shivered. Sophie opened the door.

"*Chérie*," she screeched with outstretched arms towards Jack. "*Mon petit frère!*"

So long as that's all he was. She had dreadful hands; nails like claws. And a most unbecoming "beauty spot" on the side of her chin. Probably fake.

Jack introduced us, just as I was about to make excuses for a hasty retreat. She grabbed me and led me towards the kitchen.

"Don't you think he is *the* most delicious *morçeau* in Paris? If we weren't related, I would be so tempted. But then I have Marcel."

A long, thin streaky rasher made its way round a doorway. He didn't offer a hand and barely smiled.

"He is, you know, depressed," she said, explaining.

No need to make everyone else's life a misery just the same.

"Ever since Jean-Paul died. Because Jean-Paul was going to get him published, make him into a star."

"If he has talent, I'm sure he'll make a go of it without Monsieur Sartre," I said, with just the slightest emphasis on the 'if'.

Leaning against the trendily shabby kitchen unit, she pointed her Zephrin Drouhin-shaped breasts in my direction.

"Buckets of it, he has, mark my words."

But was his talent literary? I couldn't wait till he was unleashed upon the world. After all, the skinny depressive of the pack, Beckett, is dead.

She turned towards the press and extracted a handful of assorted packets. Each was opened and sniffed. One was thrown into the bin, two were put back in the cupboard and a third was put into a saucepan with a squirt of wine and cupful of water.

"A delicious recipe my mother left me. We eat it most evenings."

That would explain skinnymalink. The body misses the croissant Saint Sartre used to give him.

"Thank you just the same, but we've eaten," I replied in response to her offer of a plate with fork, though half-sorry, as I was intrigued to know what the offering tasted like. Perhaps Jack could prove his love . . .

In the sitting-room, Skinny was explaining some profound philosophical issue to Jack. Words were coming fast and furious – at least two a minute. Jack nodded sagely, polite to a fault.

Sophie arrived with a yellow mess on top of soggy

rice, smelling and looking like three day-old scrambled eggs. I suddenly wanted home.

"I think, Jack, we'd better not interrupt Sophie's supper. Let's just gallop off to our various scratchers."

Sophie winked at Jack. The creep smiled back.

"Well, I'll away anyway," I declared. "No, don't bother – I'll grab a taxi," I said, pulling at the door handle, not even the price of a glass of water in my pocket.

However, there are some fates worse than Sophie. Fortunately, it wasn't snowing or raining but it was damn cold. And dark. I hadn't even a can of hairspray to discourage unwelcome attention. Just walk tall, pretend you'll damage them more than they can damage you.

However, Paris at night is as safe as a nudist camp. So much flesh on offer, no need for anyone to fight for it. Middle-aged women led weedy-looking foreign men down dark alleyways, reappearing half an hour later for the next customer.

In a doorway, a young girl was getting rid of her last meal: pregnancy, or perhaps a bad prawn.

Inside an hour I was inserting the key into the Lagoutes' door and creeping softly to my room. The light was on.

"I really don't know what to make of you, Philippa." Mary smiled. "You've gone to the dogs. You, who were so choosy, who wouldn't give up a night's study for a man."

I concurred. I was as confused as she was.

"I thought you had someone in tow at home," Mary pulled the covers over her.

"Must be what the frogs call a *coup de foudre*." I sat down heavily on the bed. "Never happened to me before, except in a currach off the Aran Islands, but I blamed the sun then. I can't think of any excuse for Jack." I removed my shoes which felt two sizes too small.

"However, it's all finished now. Whatever aberration I've been going through has now burnt itself out. It's back to the grindstone in the Louvre tomorrow, after all, I haven't much time left."

Mary looked at me the way my father used to: Tell us another one.

What the hell. It was all too complicated.

I lay down on my own scratcher in the corner and was asleep instantly. Long walks had their uses.

Not only was I back writing up my research with a vengeance, I had fourteen and a half pages finished before lunchtime. I was regaining my self-respect. I suppose we're all entitled to go off the rails for a day or two. The tug of war between *"coeur"* and *"raison"* is still alive and well and, reluctantly, I had to admit I too was human.

A head of Celtic hair glinted in the shafts of sunlight. I lowered my head, wished I had a hood.

"You can't escape that easily, Philippa!"

There it was again, the slight inflection at the end. I was beginning to hate the sound of my own name.

Perhaps I was beginning to hate me, for being glad to see Jack. We always blame others when it's our own damn fault.

"Not very *cordial* the way you took off. Fortunately, I have you taped. Come and share my luncheon basket with me. A trip to Fontainbleu is what you need."

Like a lamb led to the slaughter, I followed. What a lily-livered, sex-starved creature I was, *au base*.

I was ushered into a large white car with silver-work on its side. Mozart was playing on the stereo system. There was a distinct whiff of lavender in the air, the genuine article, not some chemical excrescence.

I looked at my escort to find some reason, however slight, why I was there. The head was leonine, the mouth firm but sensual and the eyes, when he looked at me, were full of . . . love.

I turned quickly and stared at the road. His hand crept towards mine; it felt strong and honest. I hoped it was true that *la coeur a ses raisons que la raison ne connaît pas*. Otherwise, we were all sunk.

The scenery around Fontainbleu would make you almost glad to be alive. All manner of exotics there – stag, wild boar, heron and kite. Though fewer and fewer of these remained. The Frenchman's motto is: if it moves, shoot it.

"Bit sad, are we?" Jack enquired.

"Thinking about beautiful animals being shot for no good reason," I said.

"Is there a good reason for shooting anything?"

"Well, if your children are starving with hunger. Any other reason is simply murder."

"That's a bit strong, my Philippa!"

I folded my arms and sank into my seat. Why do we expect others to understand our feelings. It would be nice if they'd even listen without overreacting.

"You never mentioned the sex kitten and her streaky rasher!" I gasped at the sight of Sophie and her paramour, stretched out on the grass, trying hard to look cool and relaxed.

"They just take time to get to know, Pips. Honest."

Jack stopped the car and I allowed myself to be brought to the merry twosome. Jack spread a rug for me. Sophie offered another yellow mess from her food flask. I took one of Jack's pies instead – pork with hard-boiled egg – and accepted a cup of claret, heavy and fruity, like the company.

"Nature at this time of year is so . . . quiet, unobtrusive," Sophie pronounced.

Dead I would have said, but Jack looked at me and I kept quiet.

"Better'n summer with the things that go buzz and sting," Jack said, politely.

He edged closer to me, his thigh pressed against mine.

"Summer is worst of all. I often feel like taking off for Antarctica." Sophie simpered.

I'd offer to pay her fare.

"Something about wastelands that's inviting,"

Streaky Rasher swallowed his glass of wine and stretched for a refill. I grabbed the bottle just in time.

"There isn't a soul there," he went on, staring at me slightly uncharitably.

"Oh, but there is," I said. "Full of explorers in various stages of disintegration, whalers and penguins. Overpopulated, in fact. And not a blade of grass anywhere."

Jack looked at me then with a mixture of criticism and consternation. I decided, once again, that flight was preferable to confrontation. Best to preserve the decencies.

"I'll wait for you in the car," I said, swallowing the last of my claret and taking the rug with me. Sometimes I wished I weren't so insightful.

"Sounds like it was some picnic," Mary said as I regaled her with my experiences from Fontainbleu and Jack's silent drive all the way back. "That Sophie one is a real pain and yer man is a bit of a bloodsucker. Wonder if she washes his underwear?"

"One of those arty types who doesn't bother wearing any," I suggested, sinking even deeper into the hot bath.

She gave me one of her appraising looks. "You'll have to let me meet this fellow of yours, Philippa. Sounds like it's serious."

"Don't be daft! A holiday romance." As soon as the words passed my lips, I knew it was a lie. Jack meant more to me than I cared to admit. A great deal more.

Monsieur and Madame had gone to a "Hot Spot" for the evening, leaving cheese and ham for supper.

"They're not bad, really, Mary." I sank my teeth into a piece of ripe Camembert on crisp French bread. "Seem generous with food." A full plate equals a kindly heart.

"That's Madame. She gives so much and Monsieur takes it all. I just wish sometimes he'd be nice to her and tell her she's pleasing him. But he's a selfish pig."

"Mary! I didn't think you knew the word."

Phone.

Mary rushed off to answer it. I finished the bread and draped the towel round my hot body.

"It's Jack, down in the hall," she returned breathlessly. "He'll be up *tout de suite*."

Wonderful.

He brought a bunch of flowers and a bottle of Pinot.

"To make up for a miserable afternoon," he said, kissing me on the mouth in full public view.

Mary ran to get the corkscrew.

I kissed him back and wondered what I ever did without such a soft mouth. I survived, I suppose. Barely.

"Which way is your bedroom?" he asked, tugging at my towel.

Later, as I led Jack through the sitting-room to the door, we passed Mary, slumped on the couch, an empty bottle by her side. However, her eyes were open; not dead but glazed.

"Bring a friend next time," she said to Jack.

"Would if I could," Jack kindly said, blew a kiss and took himself off into the night. I didn't tell him what little time I had left in Paris.

"Must be wonderful to be so desired, so wanted," Mary said, reaching for the empty bottle. "Like a good sup of wine at this minute."

"Wine never solved anything, Mary. It only makes what's bad even worse. Not to mention the headaches."

"I know, I know. Worth a try once in a while. Gives you something else to worry about. I think, Philippa – and don't laugh – I'm a lesbian."

"I wondered why you cut your hair short."

"I knew it! You make a joke of everything. But I'm serious. I want every man I see to be a woman. And I want every woman."

"One thing you must not be, Mary, is indiscriminate. Decide what sort of person you like and only settle for that. Otherwise life is an endless tunnelling for the indefinable, the elusive. Concentrate on staying sober and wise and aware."

She stared at me as if I had two heads.

"I never heard you make such a lovely speech. And you don't see anything wrong with preferring women?"

"Not a thing. So long as you don't bat your eyelids in my direction – at least, not twice."

"You're safe as a house, Philly. I've eyes only for Giselle."

I tried not to let my eyebrow climb to my hairline. "And how does Nappy feel about it all?" I enquired.

"Hasn't a clue. In fact, he'd probably be delighted. About as virile as a bedpost; used every excuse in the book from "sore back" to "sore bum" and back again. Poor Giselle used to cry herself to sleep after his rejections."

89

Neither the navy sky nor the warm air encouraged me in the slightest. I wanted to stay in bed, deny my departure. Perhaps if I were ill I could stay a day longer, put it off. But we have to face difficulties, in the end. I would always have to go home and Jack would always have to stay. Perhaps that's why we'd fallen for each other in the first place, we knew it was hopeless. Always a spur to love.

Mary silently handed me a cup of coffee. Sensitive to a fault. I squeezed her hand. I was sure I spotted a tear rolling down her cheek. Loss touches us all.

We hugged on the doorstep, patted each other's backs. I didn't trust my voice, so I nodded instead and walked down the empty stairs. Stairs I had climbed and descended so joyfully at times.

Jack was waiting outside, looking straight ahead. I got into the car and put my hand on his leg.

"My God," he croaked, "why is there such a word as 'goodbye'?"

"Because it all ends for us, finally, I suppose," I said.

"So, this is final, is it?"

The thought hadn't occurred to me. "Not in so far as we live in the same world, and we're both still alive, though separated by distance."

"That's the bit I don't like."

He slipped me a parcel at the departure gate, gave me a quick hug. And was gone. Jack. Two of the craziest weeks of my life. The plane was airborne before I had time to blow my nose. Modern travel had a lot to answer for.

Chapter Five

❧

A cry of Absence, Absence, in the heart

Eddie – ever faithful, ever dull – whisked me from the airport to the bamboo couch in a matter of minutes.

"Not just now, Eddie." I put a stop to his wandering hand. He pulled it back and sulked.

"Care to open a tin of chicken soup?" I asked. Perhaps if his hands and mouth were occupied, I wouldn't have to make excuses.

He was at the cupboard in seconds. Like a greyhound, Eddie is always hungry.

"I'll add a bit of pasta, make a meal of it."

Not for me, thank you. I chewed on a nail. Who cared about food with no Jack to share it?

The phone rang. I jumped as if stung.

"Hold on, Pips. Take it easy. I'll go."

I managed to grab it without breaking either my leg or Eddie's.

"Soup's boiling over," I said to him as I lifted the receiver, took a deep breath and prepared to husk my huskiest.

"So, you're back!"

Please God, don't do this to me. Aggie, fighting fit.

"Just." I didn't bother keeping the disappointment from my voice.

"What was it like?" she asked.

"Like nothing on earth. Paradise. And the food was good too."

"You sound like your usual self anyway."

"Why, thank you." That threw her. She decided on another tack.

"I suppose you brought back a bagful of presents."

That caused a twinge of guilt. Agatha knows the buttons to press.

"Didn't have a minute to shop. However, I got you some duty-free. Perfume," I hastily added.

That did it.

"That was short and sweet like an ass's gallop," Eddie said from behind a foul-smelling mound of spaghetti, swimming in thin chicken soup.

I passed him a glass of even thinner Beaujolais. "Sorry about the wine. Worst I've ever tasted and it's just been bottled."

He swallowed the glassful and held out for another. "Anything in *your* company tastes like nectar."

He probably saw my lip curl. He hastily added, "Couldn't agree more, Pips. The worst wines, like the worst books, get the biggest hype. Mostly."

He ladled half the spaghetti into his mouth. I took up the evening paper to shield my eyes but still heard the slurps. A lot to be said for the Plymouth Brethren who eat alone. Except for Jack. Jack. The ache was there, like a death.

"Work not go well?" Eddie enquired. "You don't seem full of the joys of whatsit."

"Eddie! I wish to goodness you'd give up those clichéd words. They're extremely irritating."

He dropped fork in mid-air; the mound of spaghetti toppled.

"Philippa! I thought . . . I sort of . . . well, that we liked each other, that you sort of . . . had some kind of feeling for me."

His mouth lay open like a disappointed child. Bad and all as I felt, I hadn't the heart to tell him about Jack.

"Not tonight, Eddie. I'm sorry." And I really meant it.

Life went from bad to infinitely worse. Jack was in every man I passed, an absence from every meal I ate. An empty bed. A heaviness when I got up and a misery when I went to sleep. Instead of healing the loss, time merely increased it. I called to see Nellie, my confidante, my emotional mother, when my true mother was too busy with her life to notice me. It was Nellie who put Savlon on my shredded knees, who poured vinegar on the wasp stings and Nellie who tucked me into bed with A A Milne's cautionary tales.

"He sounds a bit of a namby-pamby, Apple-Blossom." My pet name, derived from Pippy or Pippin – as in Cox's.

"What on earth makes you think that?" Nellie's judgments were never based on any logical connection.

"Socks. You said he wore *white* socks. Only namby-pambys wear those!"

And that was that! I didn't like to inform her that between sheets Jack was one hundred per cent male. But Nellie was an innocent. She thought sex was just a big hug with your clothes off.

"Don't mind me," she said, pouring her treacly tea into the rosebud china cup, "where I was brought up it was all dark socks – camyflages the dirt better. Dark socks, strong tea and Woodbines."

"Sounds exciting."

"None of your cheek. We had brown bread and porridge too."

I sipped my tea graciously. Nellie might be cracked but she was all I had.

She ladled raspberry jam onto a steaming scone and handed it to me.

"Suppose you'll be off to gay Paree again so. Or," she winked, "maybe he'll be coming over?"

I dropped the scone halfway to my mouth.

"Afraid there's nothing planned, Nellie. Nothing at all."

The morning proved me totally wrong. A letter from Jack:

Dear Pips

Can't stand it any more. I'm either coming to Ireland or you're coming here. I'm fed up taking cold showers. Haven't touched a morsel of food in a fortnight. Life without you is like summer without swallows, sex without an orgasm, an egg without salt – it's hell!

Help!

J

The phone rang for an age in Jack's tiny room.

"Hiya. Knew you'd phone. Heart of gold has my Pippy."

"I haven't even said hello yet!"

"I knew you by your smile."

"Been sniffing the Christian Dior again? No sooner is my back turned than you're scaling dizzier heights than that attic of yours."

His laughter practically shattered my eardrum.

"God, Pips – who needs a tonic when they've got you? Good to hear you again. I'd rather *feel* you though . . . your hand, your leg. Anything."

Silence.

"Is it as bad for you?" he asked. "I haven't even shaved since you left. Just lay in bed planning our future. There's a *propriété* going for very little more than I could sell all my bits and pieces. In the south of France, near Aix. Don't worry, there's a university there. I could finish my law studies and, seeing we wouldn't be too far from Arles, you could write the definitive work on Van Gogh and Gauguin. The place has a little vineyard and olive grove. We can live on wine and olive oil, maybe grow a few courgettes and tomatoes just for a bit of variety. Keep a goat, pr'aps . . ."

Silence.

"Pips? Anyone home? What do you think?"

"I thought for a moment I was superfluous. You seem to have everything worked out."

"Sorry. I should have asked you first. Afraid I got carried away. Does this mean, you don't think it's a good idea?"

"No."

"You mean, you think it is – a good idea?"

I let him stew for a second.

"Sort of. For a few weeks, anyway."

"You're the worst – I mean the best – torturer I know!"

Just so long as he didn't expect me to spend my time sewing flour bags to make dungarees.

"Peaches – I mean, Patricia – how about typing up my manuscript inside a fortnight? For a cheque, of course. A large cheque."

When I saw the pound notes shining back from her green eyes, I knew I was in safe hands.

"What's the rush? You're not due for another twelve weeks."

"Let's just say, I've had an offer I've decided not to refuse. I've been to see the Prof and he's given me leave of absence – to study Cézanne's *Mont Ste Victoire* series first hand. So, I'm in a bit of a rush, before the mistral ruins everything."

A gleam came into her eye. "I could do it in the evenings, after work – you could borrow Eddie's word processor. Only problem is," she batted her long lashes and bit her lip, "I need lashings of coffee. And you're so busy."

"A couple of flasks would surely fix that," I said.

"Well, I was really thinking of *fresh* coffee, made by a friend. We'd be no trouble, sleep on the floor – and your book would be *guaranteed* at the end of a fortnight."

Who was I to stand in the way of love?

Ophelia, aka Feelie, arrived in the dead of night in a diaphanous black number, revealing the little humps of her breasts, among other things.

"This is going to be awkward, Philly, working here," Feelie said, "seeing you're such a good friend of Eddie's. I'm sure he . . . visits."

"Worry thou not, Feelie," I said, "your secret's safe with me. Your brother is so taken up with the past he never sees what's in front of his eyes."

Her face fell slightly. Nothing more disappointing, when you're trying your damnedest to be a sexual rebel, than people not noticing.

Within hours Peaches had her dainty undies all over the place – part of the mating behaviour, no doubt. Feelie contented herself with looking strong and cerebral, especially over the pot of pasta she was boiling. She and "Tishy" eyed each other at least every two minutes. I almost envied them. But then I thought of Jack and when we'd be ensconced in Provence,

simmering ratatouille and sampling the *vin de pays* . . .
Though that would hardly pay the rent.

Phone.

"If it's Agatha, tell her I'm busy authoring. But get
her phone number," I shouted to Feelie's back.

"It's Eddie," a red-faced Feelie whispered.

"Why shouldn't she be here?" I to an incredulous
Eddie. "She's busy making coffee for Patricia. Of course
you may."

"Afraid he's coming round," I informed the ladies.
Feelie put a hand over her mouth; Peaches shrugged
her shoulders.

"What's the problem, Ophie?" Peaches asked. "It's
not as if there's a risk of pregnancy, AIDS or VD."

Sounded positively healthy.

Eddie arrived as we were in the middle of working out a
particularly tricky section of the book. He looked from
Feelie and Peaches, shook his head, looked at me,
shook his head again and sat down heavily. Feelie was
in the middle of explaining the Van Goghs, her PhD in
Botany proving invaluable.

"Those potatoes in *The Potato Eaters*, Philippa, they
are a special variety imported into Holland in the
1850s, said to survive potato blight. The Irish wouldn't
buy them as seed because they were too expensive.
Remember they used to save their own."

Eddie showed a glimmer of interest and joined his
head to ours, looking at the painting.

"Well," Feelie continued, "that variety would never

have been eaten by peasants at this time. Only the rich could afford potatoes after blight decimated the crops in Europe. So, Van Gogh is really painting with a rich man's memory. The picture's a lie."

"Gosh, Ophie, you're such an expert," Peaches gushed. Feelie blushed. Eddie shifted his bottom and asked, "Coffee anyone?"

But Feelie's mind was travelling on. "And look at this, Pippy. See the grain the gleaners are busy collecting? Well, that grain is a figment of the artist's imagination. There is no cereal on earth which has a seed-head like that. Not even the grain they took from the mummy's tomb. So," she said, spreading the pictures on the table, "while Vincent may have been a champion of the poor, he never guddled in their chores. A couch socialist. World is full of them!"

Eddie looked at his sister almost admiringly. "That sounds like a good title for a book, Ophelia," he said.

"World is full of them?"

"No! *The Couch Socialist*. Easy to tell everyone else what to do, rather than do it yourself. And," he looked slightly embarrassed, "perhaps Peaches would type it for you."

Thus giving the brotherly imprimatur to their relationship.

I decided it was time for a nightcap. In the cool of the kitchen, I pondered Feelie's revelations. I could ignore them and save myself much rewriting. No one would be any the wiser. Unlikely a botanist as knowledgeable as Feelie would scrutinise my findings to that extent.

I poured four generous tots of the best Scotch, filled the glasses with hot water and tossed in twists of lemon, studded with cloves.

Of course, conscience doth make cowards of us all. I would have to work through the night.

"Can I give you a hand?" Eddie asked. I handed him the tray.

"Nightcap time. I've a long one ahead of me."

"Thought you'd never say that!" Eddie whispered, his arms encircling my waist. "Ever since you came back from Paris, I've been beside myself, aching for you."

Just what I didn't want to hear.

"Seriously, I've a night's work ahead – on my book."

He kicked the waste bin, twisted the tea towel into a knot and left without any farewells. I wasn't looking forward to breaking my news to him.

The girls finished the hot toddies in a twinkling and held out for another. I had a rather stiff one, and spilled my dilemma to them.

"I just can't ignore what you've told me about realism in those paintings of Van Gogh's. Either my scholarly sense of rightness or my sheer stupidity won't let me off the hook."

Ophelia nodded sagely. She knew all about dissimulation. "You'd regret it forever," she said with feeling.

"If it's of any help, Pips," Peaches, wide-eyed, said softly, "we'd be happy to stay on later."

I smiled my thanks and rushed to refill the glasses in case they saw my tears of gratitude. Never does to let people see what a softie you are.

Peaches typed my additions and corrections into the small hours while Feelie dished up tasty morsels and brewed mugs of tea. I went to bed. Sleep, however, was not to be. I was awakened by a slight creak, like the bamboo couch blowing in the wind, which soon worked itself up into a howling gale. Added to the cacophony of the squeaks was the worry of bamboo fatigue. I sat up in the dark. Which vase should I break to stop the momentum? Perhaps if I went to the bathroom? And then my milk of human kindness got the better of me. Poor girls, starved of love, did they not deserve this hour together? But what about me? I protested to this kind voice. Am I not entitled to a little shut-eye?

I bounded out of bed, through the door and into the sitting-room. Feelie turned at the open door, her mouth open in consternation, her hand rushing to cover what, to an innocent in these matters, looked like a unicorn's horn strapped to her navel.

"It's the couch I'm worried about," I lied. The trauma to Peaches's tissues from a blunt object concerned me too. What if she couldn't sit at the word processor? "See those little mounds of dust under the joints? Woodworm droppings. The whole thing probably has as many holes as a Malteser. Quite a jolt, if it collapses."

Silently, I pulled down the futon, threw on a pair of sheets and a rug.

"There," I said, "that should be a bit more comfortable – not so far to fall. Breakfast is at eight."

There wasn't a sound for the rest of the night.

Chapter Six

❧

Four legs bad; two legs even worse

Lightweight suits and expensive aftershave filled the plane from Paris to Marseilles. A dish of *al dente* pasta with tomato sauce, heavily laced with basil, and accompanied by an earthy Cahors put me at ease with the world and helped knock my misgivings out of focus.

Aggie had bid me a tearful farewell. One half of me was grateful anyone felt that strongly about my departure while the other, slightly jaundiced, half had a sense that she would merely miss the squeal of her faithful pin-cushion.

Her parting gift was a surprise – a pair of heavy-duty gloves. "So your hands don't get stained with grape juice," she said.

"Does this mean we can expect to see you at the grape harvest?" I asked as neutrally as I could possibly manage. "Don't forget," I said, as I pushed my hand into a glove, "it takes at least six months for the wine to be drinkable – even by you."

She turned tail without a backward glance. Perhaps I too would miss the odd jab at a pin-cushion.

Peaches and Feelie had said their goodbyes earlier. Grateful for being allowed to rent my mews while I was sorting out my life elsewhere, they cooked an early breakfast. However, very *Brut* champers and dry, leathery sausage with scrambled egg at six in the morning are not for the faint-hearted.

"By the way," I warned, "if you see old Georgie guddling in a yellow bucket in the dead of night, stay inside – and keep the windows shut."

They looked at me as if I had several heads.

A wall of kerosene, oil and earth greeted our descent from the plane. I gave myself a quick spray of bergamot and soldiered forth. What if Jack took one look at me and decided Philippa in Paris was merely a dream and Provence is reality? That my mere 36C *embonpoint*, tight bottom and multiple-orgasmic undercarriage had suddenly lost their lustre in the Provencal sun? What if he wanted marriage, children, merely a slave in the vineyard while he sorted through his daddy's papers?

"Wired to the moon as usual, Pips. Least you could do is *pretend* you're pleased to see me," Jack greeted me.

"Must be the cold – or something," I said, not wishing to confess my fears. Of course, as soon as I looked at him, they vanished. It was just like a cheap romantic tale – I actually felt happy. And all thanks to a man! God has a lot to answer for.

"That's better, Pips!" His hurt eyes changed to

something more joyful. He grabbed my suitcases. "Let's just take it easy. Softly, softly." He planted a moist kiss on my mouth. It felt like more. "I fancy a cool something or other – how about you?"

My look said it all.

Several cool somethings later, we were glued to each other as if he were about to depart on a secret mission to Bosnia.

"You'll love the little pile I found for us. Over 300 years old! Character written all over it."

Usually synonymous with crumbling plaster and weak foundations.

"I had it surveyed. Nothing *major* needs fixing. Just the odd slap of paint here and there. The views are magnificent. Bit chilly this time of year, they say it's not usually as cool. But you'll love it. And I've got a surprise for you."

I could hardly wait.

In the event, I had to wait another day. Jack was too unsteady on his feet to drive to the hills and I refused to motor on the wrong side of the road. We stayed at a *pension* on the Marseilles waterfront, obviously used by the ladies of the town, if the bumps, bangs and grunts on the other side of the wall were anything to go by.

"It's just not possible that the same person has been carrying on like that for three hours." Unable to sleep, I finally sat up and hugged my knees.

Jack stirred. "You're just jealous. You Irish are all the same. Must be the damp short-circuiting the nerve ends. Here, in the hot South, anything is possible. Want to try?"

Earlier we had both collapsed from too much partying and no food. Togetherness was the last thing on our minds, though I thought Jack could at least have made some sort of gesture.

He pulled back the sheet. I felt I ought to make an excuse – in deference to female modesty and cultural mores about being over-eager. But desire got the better of me.

Slightly overhung, and somewhat bruised, we arrived at the tiny village of Aigue in the Luberon hills. The *patissier*, sitting on a stool outside his shop, waved at Jack as we passed. A donkey climbed up the steep slope ahead, its cart filled with twigs.

"Vine prunings," Jack informed. "This time of year they cut off all the bits that have fruited. 'Course, the harvest is long since over. They're just finished making the wine now, bottling it soon. A good time to buy, before they put it in the cellars. Cheaper, because of the labour."

"I think I can work that out for myself." Nothing worse than having your brain programmed for you. Half the fun is piecing the information together. I was dying to know what they did with the prunings but didn't ask.

Jack sniffed. "You probably don't want to know what they do with the prunings, either."

Half a mile from the village, a left turn brought an even steeper climb towards the sky, on a track fit only for mules. Its red earth was studded with sharp stones which wanted to embed themselves in the tyres and, when frustrated, flew off at all angles instead.

"Hope there's no one behind those hedges innocently milking a goat or trimming a vine," I said.

Jack looked at me.

"And don't, for God's sake, take your eyes off the track!"

Jack laughed. "Gosh," he said, wiping the tears from his eyes, "you're priceless. The mad Irishwoman. I sure got myself into one helluva mess!"

It was the laughter that got to me. As if I were some sort of oddity, when thousands would give their eye-teeth for an hour in my presence.

"That's it, Jack. You may turn and drop me back to Marseilles. Before we fall out. Terminally."

He ignored me, continued to make disgusting gurgling noises and even stepped on the accelerator.

"If you think," he said, gasping for air, "for one instant, I can stop on this slope, let alone turn round, you're crazier 'n a mad hornet."

Just then we reached the top. The car spat a few more loose stones and came to a standstill in front of everyone's dream of a Provencal house.

"The round part at the back is the granary. The long bit next to it is the byre – that's where my surprise awaits you. And then that bit with the chimney and

107

tiny windows is the bit for living in. The tacked-on bit is the larder – of course, there's a cellar underneath."

He lifted my hand to his mouth. "Well?"

"It's just . . ." Every description I could think of sounded like a cliché in my head. "Wonderful," was all I could muster.

Jack looked disappointed, so I roused myself.

"I just love the red roof tiles and the vine growing over the porch and the way the sun seems to make it look so warm and cosy – and the view!"

He kissed me then, a long kiss with full, hot lips.

"Come on. It's even warmer inside."

Not a word of a lie. We walked through a Van Gogh yellow door into a freshly-whitened hallway. The thick stone walls kept the heat at bay and cooled the inside to the temperature of an Irish November, without the damp.

"You've been busy with a brush," I said to Jack.

"All a bit grubby when I arrived, as if a herd of bullocks had stampeded through the place and left their visiting cards. We can change the colour, no problem."

"I love it, just as it is." And I was beginning to love Jack's consideration for me, his attempts to please me. What a girl wouldn't do for someone like that!

"This is the boudoir." Jack opened the door with a flourish.

The wooden floor was broken up with scattered rugs, an armoire and a scrubbed pine washstand. A large bunch of lavender sat on the windowsill and perfumed the room. The bed had carved mahogany ends and a bright yellow Provencal quilt.

"Welcome home," Jack whispered between breaths. I opened to him like a giant Peruvian lily welcomes the bee to fertilise it; though, unlike the lily, I let him go, eventually.

"What do you think of it?" he asked.

"That's a very rude question just at this particular moment."

"The house! Farm! Ambiance!"

"Oh!" I smiled. "My dream home. Everything a girl could have wished for."

That did it.

Two hours later we attended to other needs. The kitchen was down a flight of steps and above another, which led to the cellar. It was out on a limb, resting on pillars with a veranda looking towards the Luberon Hills and capturing the evening sun. The vegetable rack held enough for a giant ratatouille. Jack handed me two very phallic courgettes, an aubergine and a not-very-sharp knife.

"The previous owners left their garden in mid-production. They had a 'total and irreversible falling-out', according to the estate agent. Something to do with not having children. She wanted loadsa and he wanted none. Heavy into astrology and fairies and gnomes. That's what all the star signs are about."

Sure enough, every wall was covered with some sort of symbol.

"Typical, of course; when you can't stand the pain of

the present, you invent a fantasy world to live by. It's everywhere. Aggie in love with the booze, Eddie swears he's in love with me and thinks I'm his world."

"Perhaps you are. Don't be so harsh. We all need something." He wiped the onion tears from his eyes.

"What we all need is a swift kick in the pants." I dispatched both courgettes into the ratatouille pan. "The only reality is that the world continues, that life is constant change and that we will die. All these little fantasy worlds stop us thinking about the important things. Facing up to what life means."

Jack stopped in mid-chop.

"I suddenly don't feel hungry. What's the point in it all. We'll just die one day."

"The point is, dear Jack," I said, waving my blunt knife in midair, "we face the challenge of what we're given. No ifs, ands or buts. No thinking we've the winning numbers in the lottery – but just not *this* week. We'll be happy *just as soon as* this, that or the other happens. Life is *now*. This instant. This moment. We could be dead tonight. By the by, where's the nearest nuclear reactor?"

"Thought of that. Two hundred miles away; not that it's far enough if it blows up, but we can jump in the car, get to Marseilles and a plane to the other side of the globe."

Jack chopped the tomatoes. Deep red, firm but oozing with juice. I put the aubergines into the pot with a ladleful of deep green olive oil from a wooden container.

"Anyway, Pips, let's just have a *petit verre* to cheer

ourselves up. If we're gonna die, we may as well be as numb as possible."

And then that laugh that almost shredded the tomatoes.

He led me towards the sitting-room, two glasses in one hand and a nameless bottle of wine in the other. He was keeping the best room till last, cosy and comfortable, though the ceiling was so low I had to make for the yellow couch *ventre à terre*. The oak beams were beautiful but made for midgets. Jack, being smaller, had no difficulty.

"Your actual French window," Jack said, opening it to sounds of gurgling water. "A little stream, too. The spring rises the far side of the house and pours down this side. Great gusher of a thing that eventually feeds into the Durance. They must have used it to turn a millstone in what's now the byre. I found an old stone there. You'll see it in the hall. Helluva job lifting it. Used old Neddy to drag it."

"Old Neddy? Where on earth is he? Won't he be looking for his dinner? Here's us having a gay old time and the poor old donkey half-starved!"

"Hang on, Pips! He's got a field full of stuff and I gave him half a loaf this morning." He refilled his glass, tossed back the contents and poured another. "Thought I'd only got myself to answer to. Seems I've you, too! Looks like I married my mother, just like every other guy in the world. You think it's love but it's just stupidity."

"If that's how you feel after a mere question, then

you can take me straight back to Marseilles. I had a good life that I left – for no good reason, it seems. I can quite easily go back to it."

Silence. Except for the gurgle of the stream.

"I know you could, Pippy," he sat beside me. "But I'd like you to stay. All this is nothing without you."

Life has some wonderful moments. A shame we've to drag them out of people.

I cast my eyes around the room. Slabs of plaster had disappeared, revealing the stonework beneath. Generations of spiders had built their stately mansions and holiday homes between the oak beams.

"Don't worry, Pips. Quick dose of DDT and we'll be rid of that lot. Thought I'd better see to the outside before winter set in. When the mistral blows we can keep warm – I mean, occupy ourselves inside."

My Buddhist nature revolted. "If you so much as harm a spidery leg, I'll have your hide for a hatband."

That laugh again. It began like a thousand castanets and ended like water going out a plughole. Nothing so lonesome as not sharing someone else's joke.

"My gosh, Pips! You'll be the death of me! Where do you get the lines? You'd go down a treat in New York. They'd even pay money to listen to something fresh."

"The only problem, Jack, is that I'm not joking."

"But that's what makes you so cool."

If I didn't hitch up the donkey and cart and head for Marseilles airport there and then, I never would. I sank back into the couch and thought about the morning.

Life at the highly unoriginally named *Mon Rêve* – I voted for *L'Espoir* but was shot down as being too despairing – began at 5.30 am. Three goats came to the back door to give themselves up for milking. A motley crew, one black, one brown and one mixture. Their udders hung like long Conference pears, almost touching the ground.

"Makes them susceptible to barbed wire," Jack said. "See, Brownie has only one teat. They said so on the list of *Animaux de Ferme* the estate agent gave me. Seems she lost it to the dog who, fortunately for us, has gone to his happy whatchamacallit. That's his burial mound, on the bend in the road from which he used to spring to bite at the postman's ankles."

Neither the mental anguish of Van Gogh nor the drama of Gauguin could compare to the happenings at *Mon Rêve*, it seemed. Life in all its gory.

Jack disappeared into the byre and emerged with a collection of stainless steel buckets.

"OK, Pips. This is it. You want milk in your coffee, hook up one of them there goaties and fill the pail."

"What about poor one-teated Brownie?"

"Easier to start with one than two."

How could I have been so stupid!

"So, this is your 'surprise'?"

"Clean forgot! Come to me, my sweetheart."

He pulled my arm.

"Now, close those peepers. Ah, ah! Trust me."

I left the merest sliver open.

He led me into the byre, over a stall of deep straw.

"*Eh bien*, open 'em."

They moved at that instant. Inside a cage made of twigs and twine were two golden hens with red combs. They shook their dangly bits at me.

"Well, say something!"

For once, I was speechless. They were the most beautiful things I had ever seen. Every feather just so, lying one beyond the other. And eyes that didn't waver, that stared fixedly. Beak at the ready. The darker one lifted a foot, stuck a toe in an ear and scratched like mad. The other pecked at the straw.

"Guess I'll just have to be satisfied with your smile. Whatya gonna call 'em?"

What else but Hetty and Harriet?

"Let them out, let them out!" I squealed like a child.

Jack hesitated. "You sure?"

I pulled the long stick holding the doors of the cage together. As one, they shot out, wings spread, feathers flying.

"They'll be basking on the Côte d'Azur in no time!"

"Catch them, you idiot! Catch them!" I could barely get the words out. My throat tightened at the possibilities my internal cinema brought forth – massacred on the road by a garlic-chewing *petit bourgeois* on a bicycle, stampeded by a herd of goats, shot by the local animal-lovers who do it "for fun".

"Hang on, Pips, hang on!" Jack's face matched the hens' combs. "Here, you grab the dish of food, bash it on the ground. Maybe they're hungry."

I did as I was told, though I'd have preferred to hitch up the donkey and grab the butterfly net. Het and Har had disappeared into the undergrowth.

However, no sooner had the din of the dish echoed across the hills than two golden shapes came towards me. Gingerly. Like girls making their first ballroom entrance. Heads cocked this way and that. Toes placed tentatively forward.

"Easy now," Jack whispered.

I reduced the din to a mere jingle. Onward they came. My sweaty hands almost lost the dish. A beak stretched towards it. And another. In the split second before they realised the dish was empty, Jack dived towards them, scooped them up in a blaze of feathers, dust, feet and squawks.

I clapped.

Not what was required.

"For God's sake do something!" he yelled.

I searched for something to grab but failed. The whole collection was in constant motion. I found a leg, worried about pulling it off, let it go, grabbed another and another and soon I had four. I carried them to the barn, wings beating against my legs. Two very angry girls. I bundled them into the cage, shoved in the stick and let them sort themselves out.

"Now, girls," I said when I caught my breath. "Was it all worth it? Just be a little more circumspect in future."

I looked out the barn door. Jack was still prostrate.

"Anyone alive?" I enquired.

A cough. I ran towards him. "Got them behind bars again."

Another cough.

"Do you think, Pips, it's too early for our lunchtime aperitif?"

"Of course not."

Anyone who bought me such beautiful hens could have anything they wanted. Within reason.

Except that, after a long, cool glass or two of Provencal *rosé* we were rendered completely useless. While it's simple and straightforward, with a heavy accent on the taste of almonds, the truly wonderful thing about Provencal *rosé* is its inability to confer a hangover. Jack and I appreciated this particularly. It's one thing to indulge oneself and quite another to have to pay for it later.

We still had the goats to milk.

"Think I'll forego milk in my coffee. Learn to do without," I said.

"Fine. But the goats have to be milked or they swell up and get mastitis."

I lured one-teated Brownie towards me with a bucket of slug-damaged lettuce leaves, beetroot skins and rancid butter. She was not impressed. However, just before she decided to wander off, I had the halter round her neck and led her, toes digging into the dusty soil, towards the milking site. Jack was already leaning against Whitie, squirting milk into a bucket for all he was worth. It looked simple enough.

I grabbed the single teat and got a kick on the wrist for my audacity.

Jack laughed.

"It's all right for you, you've had several week's start."

"It's just that I got the same treatment. Brownie is not the most courteous of people. Not like Whitie here. A lady."

I offered a lettuce leaf and grabbed the teat again. She jumped forward and got a hoof in the bucket. Nothing for it. I grabbed her leg with one hand and the teat with the other and squeezed. Nothing. I squeezed again. Another attempted kick. But I had the measure of her. If only I had three arms.

Another laugh from Jack. That man could be really trying. If he wasn't so good in bed . . .

"You've to kinda get the lower part of the teat filled and then pull down on it, and hey presto."

I didn't doubt it. How on earth one would manage two teats beggared belief.

I did as I was told. It worked! After a fashion. At least I got something, as well as another kick. Sweat dripped from my armpits. My trousers felt tight. I wanted to scratch where I couldn't reach. Jack's bucket was almost full. I had run out of lettuce.

"Here, let me give you a hand," he said at last.

He held Brownie while I tried to extricate the milk with both hands. And, shortly, it happened. An actual squirting sound in the bucket.

"You've done it, Pips! We'll make a farmer of you yet."

Louise Couper

That was just what frightened the wits out of me.

Jack had scrubbed the dairy till it looked sparkling clean. On one wall, the shelving held several pans for the milk: one with yoghurt fermenting, one for cheese and whatever was left was put into the butter barrel. The latter was fortunately rigged up to electricity in a labyrinth of wires. Jack peered inside.

"Enough there to get us a bit of butter for breakfast."

The finding of a lost Monet or collection of Jane Austen's letters were evidently as nothing compared to the excitement of making our own yoghurt, cheese and butter.

The barrel turned and turned and shuddered until it seemed as if the wood might splinter, but stopped after five minutes. Jack took out the bung and peered inside.

"That's it! Nice little collection of nuggets."

I scraped the ragged golden pieces from the barrel and put them on the board. He handed me the butter pats and poured the buttermilk into a glass jar.

"That's for the brown bread," he said. "You work a bit of salt into the butter as you mash it into shape with the pats."

I finally had a sort of squarish-rectangular shape with artistic edges. I marked it with a large P.

We brought the yoghurt, butter and some soft cheese Jack scraped from a muslin bag, all dripped out from the previous evening, into the kitchen. Breakfast was beginning to look promising.

"Almost there." Jack shovelled the last of the coffee

118

beans into the hand grinder. "Much better than electrically done. Keeps its flavour better."

Keep telling yourself that, and you end up having meals in arrears.

"A few strawberries in the cheese and we're done. Oh, my gosh! Clean forgot. The bread."

"Don't tell me I've to mill the grain myself!"

"Nope. Not unless you really need the exercise. Back in a truss." The car disappeared down the steep track like a stampeding buffalo.

I poured the boiling water on to the coffee grinds sitting in the bottom of a muslin square, tied on to four pieces of wood. None of your expensive, throwaway coffee filters. All was renewable, recyclable. And hard work. I made a mental note to leave the rinsing of the filters to Jack, who seemed to know all about them. No wonder the Yanks spread across the prairies like a virus. They had life taped.

The squeal of brakes announced the bread.

"Nothing like it fresh from the oven. Must try and get the recipe from the baker and we can make our own."

"Perhaps, Jack, we ought to leave some expertise to the locals. Otherwise they'll feel alienated from us, their centuries of bread-baking counting for nought."

He looked at me.

"Couldn't be you'd just prefer not to bake your own?"

"Jack, you shock me at times." With your insight.

I spread the cloth, put out the freshly-made butter,

the still-warm goat's milk, cheese with strawberries and sliced the crusty bread. Only two hours since we got up. At this rate, lunch would be sometime next week, Christmas celebrated in summer, just as soon as the vine fruits had shrivelled sufficiently.

"Tuck in, Pips!"

I didn't need encouragement. The bright yellow butter, white cheese and red strawberries looked very fetching on the way to my mouth. But there the attraction ended.

"Something wrong?"

I ran for the bathroom. Jack followed, his mouth full of baguette, ruined by rancid butter and goaty cheese.

"Gosh, Pips. Not morning sickness already!"

Very *drôle*. I looked at him. "Of all the foul-tasting items I have eaten in my time, that takes the prize."

"Then you never had sheep's eyes or bull's pizzle."

"They're weird things given to tourists. I'm talking about mundane, ordinary things like butter and cream cheese. Looks like I'll have to live on fruit."

He put an arm around me. "Now, now, Pips. It just takes getting used to proper food. All that bland supermarket stuff has to be eradicated from your tastebuds' memory. Takes about six weeks."

Just as long as it takes to die from starvation.

"Maybe it's the hygiene, Jack. We need to refrigerate the milk, pasteurise it."

"Do that, and the bugs don't work. No. No. Just persevere. Tell you what: just have the strawberries, bread and coffee for today. To keep your strength up. You'll need it out in the fields."

Wonderful. A hot, dusty library was suddenly hugely attractive. Even a seminar of bored students.

"On second thoughts, Jack, maybe I ought to give that butter another chance."

"That's m'girl! Knew you'd spunk."

Just as he was giving me an encouraging slap on the back, there was a noise like an earthquake.

"Goddam! Those two again. I suppose they *did* look after the place while I fetched you from Marseilles."

Without explanation, Jack strode out the half-door towards a collection of wheels and planks in a dust cloud. A pair of Obelix and Asterix look-alikes climbed down from the cart. Obelix sported a thick plait, tied with a piece of string.

"Bloody hell! I need a drink!" she wobbled at Jack. "Oh, you've arrived," she stared down her nose at me. "Great to have another woman around." She emphasised "woman" and wiggled at the men. My guess was they hadn't noticed what she was. She grabbed Jack's arm and steered him towards the half-door.

"Doris, from Scarborough," Jack shouted by way of explanation.

I turned to Asterix. Busy excavating his beard. Beam me up, Scottie.

"You're it, then?" he grinned. A real charmer. I gave him one of my withering looks. He must have been short-sighted. "The bird," he said.

There was a time when I would have simpered and pretended nothing was more natural or normal than to be so called. No more. I turned towards the house.

"Jacko *said* you were a bit uppitty." He sniggered, bent his grubby fingers to excavate his long greasy hair.

"Jacko" had a lot of explaining to do.

Doris and Jacko were *tête-à-tête* on the couch, an almost empty bottle of wine between them.

"I'm sure Philippa would love to hear all this, Doris," Jack said.

My withering looks were as nothing compared to Doris's. Every sinew, muscle and lump of gristle was trained to perfection, despite the flab – indeed, enhanced by it.

"Looks to me as if Doris doesn't want to tell, Jacko." I emphasised the "o". And quickly left the room.

"Pips! Wait!" Jack followed. Deliriously happy in my moment of power, I almost ran to the bedroom and had my Walkman plugged in as Jack caught up.

"Come on, Pips! Give us a hand with these two loopers. Last time they stayed two whole days."

I made *unable to hear* signs.

He slammed the door behind him.

It was dark when Jack came back. I was wide awake, watching the cockroaches scurrying about the floor.

"Thanks a lot, Philippa. Thought we were in this together, a bit of support for each other – or something like that. But no. When the going gets tough, Philippa runs off."

"Have they gone?"

"Of course not! Does a tiger quit the still-warm carcass, even when it's full?"

"Don't be so lily-livered. Tell them it doesn't suit, that we're busy, that I've got thrush. Anything, Jacko!"

"What the hell is this 'Jacko' business? Come on, out with it!"

"He of the greasy mane and festering armpits said how 'Jacko' had told them I was 'uppitty'. Deny it, if you will!"

"Why believe a stinker 'for a start' and for a second, sure I told them you were 'uppitty' and didn't hold with all-night partying. I said it in the hope they'd be scared off. Fat chance!"

I didn't apologise for jumping to conclusions. Relent and you've had your chips.

"'Cept I hadn't counted on them ignoring you and latching on to me even more."

He came closer, looked into my steely blues. "Philippa, please get rid of them. I know you're a really nice person and wouldn't know what nastiness is, much less stoop to say anything nasty but, if you wouldn't mind, get them out of here, please."

He collapsed on to the bed. I pulled the duvet over him.

"I'll do my best, Jack – I mean my worst."

Not, of course, that I'd know how. But such pleading couldn't be ignored.

Chapter Seven

❧

O, let me not be mad, mad, sweet heaven

I steadied myself against the door frame. A rather rowdy altercation was taking place.

"What would *you* know about feelings? Your acquaintance with them stopped when you slid from your mother's giant . . ."

I opened the door. Doris was standing, arms akimbo, facing down the terrified figure of her beau. He leapt when he saw me.

"Dorrie and I just having a slight disagreement," he said. "You know what it's like."

Knowing what *she's* like was enough. The man had my sympathy. Well, a tiny shred.

"I suppose – I never caught your name . . ."

"Asterix."

I gave a very respectful bow to my instincts.

"Yes, Asterix, as I was saying, or about to say, I suppose life is different for everyone."

"We're just a bit strung out. Been to what they

called an Encounter Group – to help us take stock, see where our lives were going, that sort of thing."

Doris blew her nose. Loudly. I poured myself the dregs from a bottle of our best *rosé* and sat by the window, sniffing the evening air, heavy with lavender and warm earth.

"Sounds exciting," I encouraged.

"It was. Full of crazies. All talking about their childhoods and how scared they felt 'exposing' themselves. One of them had her mother 'in the chair', but I couldn't see anything."

Doris, having examined the contents of her hankie, came to life. "Let sleeping dogs lie, that's what I say. If you're happy being fat, then why not stay that way?" she said.

"Dorrie's right. Where's the fun knowing yourself, why you do things? Life is for living. None of this negative emotional crap."

Dorrie nodded vigorously. "As I said to them, 'I'm fine, thank you very much.' I've no intention of paying money to be with a gang of crazy people talking to rabbits or dead fathers."

"Where, Asterix, did all this excitement take place? How much was it?"

"Down on the coast. Cannes. Run by two Americans. Forty dollars for the weekend, including a veggie burger with coleslaw and coffee twice a day."

"Cheaper than staying at home."

They both stared at me.

"Jack wouldn't have anything to do with it," Ast

Louise Couper

informed me. "He said it might help Dorrie but normal people had work to do, like milk goats."

I didn't say a word.

"Wouldn't advise it, if I were you. You come away feeling much worse than you went," Dorrie warned.

They climbed into their van and, without a backward glance, tore down the hill in a cloud of dust. That just about summed them up.

"This self-examination business sounds exciting," I said to Jack as we made our way to the milking parlour a few hours later.

"You're joking! What's the point in it? Whatever's there has been there so long that the groove is worn too deep. Better off learning something useful like woodcarving."

Except that it didn't sound nearly as interesting. I opened the door for the three ladies whose udders were trailing the ground with two hours' extra milk.

"I just feel I'd like to know where my life is going, Jack. One day I'm a semi-discontented art historian, and the next I'm milking goats in a run-down villa in the south of France. I feel out of control, as if I'm just reacting to events, not taking charge. I'd just like to know what's going on."

His eyes went dark with fear. "Maybe I'm scared you'll think you made a big mistake."

I didn't try to wrestle with his fear. Perhaps he was right. Not knowing was the bugbear, unlike Blackie, Brownie and Whitie whose days held the same

126

predictable pattern. Any alteration would simply mystify them.

"Let's try to have everything as clean as possible," I suggested and filled a pail with steaming water. "While rancid butter may have its adherents, looking at no one in particular, I think the tasty, creamy variety is more healthy."

"Sure, Pips, anything for a quiet life."

We sounded like an old married couple already.

In the end, Jack came with me. He said he didn't trust my driving skills on the road to Cannes. Nothing to do with love, of course.

We brought a picnic. Less-rancid-than-usual butter, hard bread, smelly cheese relieved by a basket of cherries bursting with juice. I ate these and swigged at the wine.

"Steady on. You won't be able to say your name if you carry on with that stuff."

"Mind your own business and I'll mind mine, kiss your own boyfriend and I'll kiss mine." I took another swig.

"*Charmant!*" he said, and spat out a cherry stone with force.

"You almost shattered the dials with that one, Jacko."

"Better mind your own dial then."

Jack – given to violent fugues? Come back, Eddie, all is forgiven. A ton of boredom is better than a scintilla of violence.

We drove on in silence, past fields of lavender which were here pale mauve and there a deep shade of purple. Experimenting and mixing varieties to get the best production of oil. They needn't bother for me. Oil of lavender gives me a headache.

The bottle of wine was soon empty. I suggested we stop "for refreshments", which request was met with a stony silence. I suddenly realised I hated, had always hated, red hair. And Jack's hair seemed to be even redder than red.

"Ever think of dyeing it?" I pointed to his red mop.

"Maybe this self-examination stuff isn't such a bad idea, after all," he said. "Maybe," he ran his fingers through his hair, "it's even a good idea."

At *L'Etoile*, one of the three largest hotels on the main street in Cannes, we followed the signs for "Therapy Group". We were late. About a dozen people were seated in a circle. The one with the badge was obviously the leader. He gestured to a bunch of chairs.

"Al," he said.

"Philippa – and this is Jack." Jack gave me a dirty look for not allowing him to speak up for himself.

"We're just talking about responsibility," Al said, as he looked at each of us in turn.

His partner, Arlene, smiled a welcome, creasing the masses of crinkles on her face.

"Hi, Jack," she said, ignoring me. "Care to tell us a little about yourself? Why you've come?"

Jack refused. Said it was all a bit weird and anyway he didn't want anyone to know anything about him, especially when he didn't know anything about them.

Al simply nodded. "We'll just carry on, then," he said. "Now, when I say I'm gonna take responsibility for my actions or feelings, I'm saying it's me who's doing or feeling. It's nothing to do with you, or you, or you." He pointed at each of us in turn.

"But it's often because of someone else that we feel angry or upset." Jack said, visibly angry and upset.

Al seemed delighted with this challenge and smiled broadly.

"Sure, Jack. I guess I 'made you' a little angry just now – but it's you who's feeling the anger!" he said, a trifle triumphantly, I felt.

"Hold on a second, Al. Jack is just trying to clarify something." I found myself piping up.

This was meat and drink to old Al. He tugged at his beard enthusiastically. Arlene nodded like a clockwork toy.

A bespectacled, overweight, dark-skinned person of the male persuasion put his oar in. "No need to come on at old Al so heavy, there. He's just trying to explain what taking responsibility means."

Then all hell broke loose. Fingers pointed, heads nodded and feet clattered on the floor. Jack indicated the door with his head. However, I was riveted. I wasn't moving. This was better than *Coronation Street*. Jack had had enough and was out the door quick as a flash.

Then, suddenly, you could hear a pin drop, a set of false teeth clatter, people breathing.

A tiny, bony-faced gentleman with a pencil moustache – to match his eyebrows – giggled.

"Would you care to say where you're at, at this moment, Don?" Al asked him.

The moustache quivered. A size eighteen lady, with breasts almost touching her knees, spoke. "The guy's obviously laughing at *me*. Been the same since I was knee high to a grasshopper." She began to cry. Sob. "Matter of fact," she wiped her nose on her sleeve, "no one ever took me seriously in my whole life. See these things?"

She lifted her giant mammaries for all to see, as if we hadn't. "When I cried about them to my Pop – Ma died when I was born . . ."

This didn't surprise me. Breasts in a newborn are not funny; expectant mothers should never eat hormone-fed chicken.

"Pa said: 'Dolly, don't you worry your purdy little head none. The guys will just love 'em – one in each ear!'"

There wasn't a single laugh in the room. I could have sworn I heard my heart beating.

"That wasn't a nice thing to say," Al broke the silence. "Matter of fact," Arlene added, "it was pretty insensitive."

Dolly crumpled, as elegantly as she could, amid offers of tissues, cigarettes and cups of coffee.

"Why are men such shits?" I found myself shouting, and immediately regretted it.

"Would you care to expand on that?" Arlene asked.

"Well, they are, don't you agree?"

"Let's just see where you're coming from, Philippa."

I kept my mouth firmly shut.

"It's OK if you don't want to tell us."

I wished she'd stop being so reasonable and *make* me tell her. In a way, I was dying to. But I let it pass.

"If you want to come back to it, that's no problem."

I was at bursting point. "Why do you have to sound so damn reasonable?"

Pencil moustache quivered again.

"What are you sniggering at?" I asked him.

Al moved towards me. "Now, let's just take this slowly. OK?"

I didn't say a word.

"How's your breathing?" he asked.

Now that he came to mention it, it was sort of stuck at my Adam's apple. I smiled. Al smiled. There was something really nice about him. I seemed to have a *penchant* for Americans, though Al was a little long in the tooth. My long-lost daddy figure?

"That a bit easier?" he asked. I nodded. But it soon became more difficult. Like being floored by an unexpected wave, I felt engulfed by sadness. Like the base Indian in *Othello* I dropped tears "as fast as Arabian trees their medicinal gum". Pencil moustache offered me a grey-white hankie. Al saved me from almost certain death with a box of clean tissues.

"Would you care to talk about it, Philippa?" Arlene, who seemed to be at the end of a long tunnel, enquired.

But it was like darkness trying to connect with light, an impossibility.

"Maybe if you just described it?"

"Well, it feels like being at the dark end of a long tunnel. I'm alone, sunk into a patch of blackness. Everything is far away, a shaft of light in the distance."

"That sure sounds pretty lonely. And scary. Anything you can do to reach that light? If you want to, that is."

"I'm a bit tired of the blackness now. I could get up and walk to the end of the tunnel."

"What a load of crap – tunnels and patches of light. You haven't budged from the room!" A handsome Frenchman with almost perfect English sneered at me.

"One of those shits you were talking about, Philippa." Big boobs looked meaningfully at me.

The Frenchman straightened even more. "What would you know, Madame – borrowing other people's opinions! Perhaps the big boobs are owing to the brains being there, no?"

I managed to suppress a slight grin but the others rolled around the place laughing.

Arlene was not amused. "Just a second, you guys, let's hear what Sabina has to say about all this."

We all stared at her. Silence. Except for her

sobbing. A terrible noise. I wanted to scream but my throat ached instead.

"I can't take any more of this," a tiny blonde woman dressed in white shorts and yellow T-shirt declared. "From the beginning, it's been unbearable. I came here to learn something, and instead I've been subjected to almost two hours of hell." She got up and lifted a straw bag from the back of her chair. "I won't expect a refund, Arlene. You'll need a stiff drink when these head-bangers go."

Arlene stretched out her arms. "I'd really like you to stay, Sabina. You're already learning something about yourself – that you have a little difficulty with anger, maybe. Sadness? Does that make sense?"

Sabina sat down again but cradled her bag in her arms, nursing it like a baby.

"How's that, Sabina?" Arlene asked.

"Difficult," Sabina's tiny voice answered. "Reminds me of my parents' rows when they came back from one of their 'parties'. Pop would bang and shout and Mom would cry and wail."

"And how did that affect you, Sabina?"

"You learnt to live with it, to think of it as normal. But I think it made me shy and quiet, not wanting to pretend I existed in case they started on me. But I suppose people have suffered worse things."

"It's what happened to you that's important, right now. Can you give it a little space?"

"I could, but I don't want to. If I started to cry, I'd never stop."

I sympathised with that part.

"Maybe a good time to take a break," Al said quietly.

Jack was in the hotel lobby, nursing a glass of beer and chatting to the waitress. And enjoying himself.

"You look like you've been in the wars, Pippy."

I wanted to tell him what a joy it was to see someone halfway normal, but asked for a glass of wine instead.

"That bad, was it?" he asked. I nodded.

"Know what you mean. I only came 'cos I wanted to be with you. Maybe I thought it would be different to the "Encounter Group" I got tossed into at Harvard. The Business School graduates had to take a non-academic option in final year. I put a pin in the list and what do I come up with – Self-exploration and Our Affective Nature. Full of head-bangers and a therapist who was full of 'I guess you're feeling pretty angry' every time I jiggled my leg."

"To be fair to the head-bangers, Jack, I'm not sure whether they're the sane ones exposing it all, while the real nutters keep it under wraps thinking they're OK and everyone else is crazy."

"Can't say I follow your logic there – just, please, let's get out of here."

We made it to the milking parlour just before nightfall. I was tired of the routine already. Blackie, Brownie and Whitie going to their respective stalls without as much as a "Good evening" or even "Hiya".

The same little dung pellets pouring like seeds into little heaps on the floor. Jack cursing and swearing at them; Jack brushing the little dark heaps into the drainage channel; Jack telling them how wonderful they were, what big udders, what creamy milk.

"If there's no sweet talk, there's no nothin' – bit like women!" he'd said.

And then, when the pails were full, the food eaten, the ladies sent to bed for the night, there was the endless scrubbing, wiping down, cooling of the milk. No sooner were you getting over last night's labours than the morning was upon you. Almost as unrewarding as students, except slightly smellier.

"You in a daze from all that crap in Cannes?" Jack enquired.

"It's better to be that way. If I were in full control of my faculties, I'd be on the next plane to Dublin."

I filled the feeding trough, cleaned udders, got the bucket into place and began the finger-numbing task of squirting the milk into the pail, one drop at a time.

"Jack?" I heard the plead in my voice. "I was wondering, about that woodworking class, the one you suggested might be more useful than the Cannes business, perhaps there's still time to enrol?"

Silence, except for the whoosh of milk going into the pail.

"Don't you enjoy milking goats, Philippa?"

And then that laugh. No wonder the butter was rancid.

Chapter Eight

~

Stay me with flagons, comfort me with Cherry Liqueur

"Amazing guy," Asterix said of the famous cabinet-maker in St Paul de Vence. "Last time I visited he was making cruet sets out of four-hundred-year-old olive trees."

Perhaps he wasn't much use with kitchen cupboards and bookshelves.

Asterix leaned forward earnestly. "Though he's a dab hand at shelves and presses."

Asterix and Dorrie had arrived to "give a hand" transplanting the vegetables which Jack had grown from seed. They mentioned something about halving the produce, which I didn't like the sound of, but spring was too far off to argue. The nuclear reactor could go at any moment. Jack tore up and down the vegetable patch with a 1950s rotavator while Asterix piled the loosened soil into ridges that were about as straight as a spiral staircase. Dorrie was supposed to join with me in dibbing in the plants, but a weak back and "appalling thirst" put paid to that. I found her a quiet corner at the far end of the field where she could sit with her bottle of wine and daydream undisturbed.

The damp soil was a deep brown that dried to the colour of faded tiles. And how it dried! Keeping the plants moist until they rooted was a problem. Jack had rigged up the sort of mobile watering contraption you see on Egyptian scrolls, a type of yoke, bent at the neck with a bucket slung on either side.

"If the sides are balanced, you don't notice the weight too much," he said.

I took his word for it and let him do the honours while I slopped water on the plants with a tin can and watched it disappear in seconds. Asterix shook his head.

"Pardon me for saying so, but . . ."

I knew nothing good would come after that beginning, so I didn't listen. Who in hell did Dorrie and Ast think they were, anyway! Immune to insults and stale bread, eating and drinking us out of house and home and then telling us how to run our vegetable patch!

"You were saying, Ast?" Jack, kindliness personified, encouraged.

"Just that if there's no humus, the water soaks away to the big lake in the centre of the earth."

"Yep, Ast, I gather that's the case. Pippy and I sure have a lot to learn. But that's why we're here. Look at all the fun we'd miss."

Indeed! The sun beating down on us, black

fingernails, the pleasure of Ast and Dorrie, nutters on the coast, not to mention the goats.

Jack went back to the yard to refill his buckets. I followed.

"Couldn't stand another *Sermon on the Vegetable* from that scrap of humanity." I helped undo the buckets from the yoke.

"What? Dear old Ast? Not his fault if he never fully developed." Jack put a bucket beneath the tap and turned it on.

Some critical deprivation while *in vitro*, no doubt. Like blood supply to the brain.

"I can almost hear those bad thoughts of yours, Pipsy. Don't you like him? He's got his good points – can't call them to mind right now – but I'm sure he's got something going for him, even if it's only his patchy moustache."

"You sound almost cynical, Jack."

I almost said 'as bad as me', but that would be confessing to it.

"You know what they say, Pips 'every cynic a disappointed romantic'. Suppose I'd really like him to be different, to be someone I could really get on with, yammer to. But then I remember in time that it's really my pop I'm wanting. And he was never around and now there's no chance of him being around. Life is hard."

Amen to that.

We put the filled buckets onto the yoke. Jack did a limbo beneath it while I held it as high as I could without collapsing under its weight.

I saw with horror the strain on Jack. His neck and face were a deep red and beads of perspiration broke out almost immediately on his forehead.

"For goodness sake, Jack! This is crazy. You'll kill yourself. There must be a hose."

He dropped the weight to the ground.

"Do you think for an instant, you thick Irish person, that if I had a hose, I'd be daft enough to carry on with this caper?"

"You bloody Yanks would do anything – just to prove how wonderful you were."

I gave a very theatrical "storming off", grateful to have an excuse to shirk work, the hot spring sun and tormenting company. And I didn't feel a shred of guilt, though part of me felt I ought to.

The cool of the cellar reminded me of home. I sat on the damp earth beneath the racks of rapidly diminishing bottles, cursing myself for not remembering to bring a corkscrew. Then, on the top rack, I spied the four-gallon jar, a shining brass tap at the important end. Too high up to lift down, I climbed two sets of steps, turned the tap and stuck my tongue underneath. Thick and sweet and tasted of cherries. Tasted like more. On to the shelf, I emptied a Kilner jar of peaches, held it underneath the brass tap and let it fill.

Its ingredients puzzled me. Each sip seemed nearer to discovery but, like Macbeth's dagger, faded as quickly as it was grasped. By the time the four gallons had diminished appreciably, I was none the wiser but certainly more at ease with the world. I was cool, hidden and at peace. Just the sort of conditions to create unhappiness. What on earth was I doing in the middle of the Luberon hills anyway? How much time had I spent tossing up the pros and cons of coming here? Did I even *like* goats? Was I running away from something?

Not a single answer came to me. Not surprisingly. I could almost feel my cortex going up in smoke, whatever lethal poison I was guzzling. Who cared? We'd all be dead one day. Stay me with flagons, comfort me with peaches, for I am *sick* to the teeth of love, of life. May as well stay in a cellar as anywhere else. Beckettian possibilities emerged. Lots of them. I knew then I needed help. Or water. Gallons of it. I was dying.

I ate the sloppy peaches hungrily and then started on the cherries. Halfway through these, I thought I heard a voice. Just as I was helping myself to another fistful, an apparition appeared.

"The winter rations!"

"Don't be stupid, Jack. I was only having a little snack."

"One, two and a half empty Kilner jars!"

I must have been hungrier than I thought. It'd only seemed like one.

"Enough to do a family of five for a month!"

"A slight exaggeration there, dearest," I said smugly.

I put down the remains of the cherries and tried to

think of something to say. But paralysis got the better of me.

"Christ! The Pinot!" Jack stared up at the brass tap, dripping only slightly.

I made no excuses, except to say, "Well, you invited Ast and Ob."

"You have this awesome Irish habit of giving people nicknames. It's not nice."

I felt roused now. I pulled myself into a semi-sitting.

"For your information, Jacko, *they're* not nice. They simply visit to eat and drink us out of house and home. Because they've nothing better to do. Not only that, that scrap of humanity you want me to give his full title to tried to tell us how to run our vegetable patch! They can't run their own lives and they come here and try to tell me how to run mine. No, thank you very much."

That fairly took it out of me and I was pleased to slump into numbness again.

Jack sat beside me. Helped himself to a cherry. And a slug from my Kilner jar. His hands were deep mahogany with clay. His nails ridged with dirt. I looked at his face. It seemed old and tired, yet relaxed, content.

"Sorry you feel like that about those two. To me, they're like stray dogs looking for a safe place. Suppose I felt, being human, I ought to give it to them when they came looking. I kinda ignore their criticism and greed and see the child inside screaming – for something. I don't think they know what."

"All very noble, Jack. You're obviously a far nicer person than me. However . . ."

"I can smell something bad coming!"

"However," I repeated, "they've had ample opportunity to examine their miserable lives – they could have stayed with Al and Arlene to do that. They've made a choice. They'd prefer to bitch and gripe about everything and everyone because it stops them looking at themselves!"

"Guess you've a point there, Pips."

I'd a feeling he was lying.

"Next time you're feeling generous to a fault, Jack, let me know. I might just be too busy with my woodworking career to give visitors more than five minutes."

I felt it was the end of something. The end of that cosiness when you're totally at one with the other person, breathing their breath, feeling their fears. Jack-and-Philippa was no more. It was now Jack and Philippa. Separate. Reality had intervened with a very damp squib.

"The classes start in a fortnight. I've booked us in."

The worst of the Pinot should have worn off by then.

"A very bad line for you." Jack handed me the phone, just as we were about to go goat-hunting at the crack of dawn.

A whisper I'd have recognised anywhere at the other end.

"Agatha, there's no earthly use in you carping on if I can't hear. You may just as well have phoned God."

"The south of France hasn't improved you any. You'd think all that sun and good food would have had some effect."

Should I put the phone down now, or wait till she got fed up with me?

"How *are* you, Agatha?"

I could tell, but reality ought to be confirmed every time.

"Terrible," came the reply. "Can't sleep at night. I get up in the morning feeling so depressed and miserable, I just can't seem to do anything."

"Try not drinking the night before. Sounds like a hangover to me."

"You never understood depression. I only feel better in the evenings, when I can relax."

For which, read 'guzzle'.

"I thought maybe, if it's OK with Jack, I'd come to see you. Maybe the sun and air will help. I've had a dreadful time with SADS."

Though SILLY ASS DRINKS (HERSELF) STUPID fitted to a T, fool that I am, I couldn't ignore the desperation I sensed behind the words. If Jack could put up with Ast and Dorrie, Agatha would be a mere trifle.

"Well, if you think it would help. It's a little primitive here, no luxuries of any kind and lots of hard work," I warned.

143

Louise Couper

"I'm well used to that, and of course I'll help out – as best I can."

When she wasn't prostrate with "depression", no doubt.

❧

It was one of those days when the south of France is like paradise – the air heavy with wild rosemary, earth and flowering vines, the light filtering through a barely perceptible haze – that Agatha arrived in some style into the farmyard. Her driver, a surly Breton – though I've never known any other kind – was not impressed with our dirt-track.

"*Diabolique!*" is how he described it. Jack gave him one of his smiles, offered him a "*verre*" and within minutes we were all friends for life. Except for Ag. She snarled at him, slapped money into his hand, and marched towards the kitchen door, with me in tow. I could see life was going to be fun.

"Where am I sleeping?" she asked.

I hadn't a clue. Part of me had refused to accept that Agatha was really coming, believing that her decision was merely a momentary aberration brought on by a gin too many.

"Well, it depends. If you want to really go "*à la campagne*", then we can fix up a straw mattress above the milking parlour. The smell of goat only lingers for an hour or two after the milking."

She put on her displeased look.

144

"Or," I said, the soul of sisterly love, "we can put you in any of the little rooms at the back of the house. They haven't been done up yet, but don't let that stop you. We wouldn't mind in the least if you wanted to slap on a bit of paint."

A look of pure hatred spread across her face, which I didn't blame her for in the least. I could be just as nasty as the next person when the wrong buttons are pressed.

I led her towards the narrow corridor, pointed out Jack's and my bedroom, the *"petit coin"* with its wooden seat and old-fashioned cistern, and the room we laughingly called the bathroom. A shower head hung in solitary splendour above a hole in the ground.

Agatha's "Humph" said it all. I made no excuses.

And we arrived at the first of the tiny rooms. Yellowed whitewash with children's drawings. Stick figures with sad faces. I always felt miserable here, a sense of loss strangled my throat.

Agatha sensed something too. "A lonely room," she said, "I think I'd prefer the stable," which made me feel even worse. She preferred the ripe smell of goat dung to all-pervading misery. No point in stirring the pot.

However, the hayloft didn't look too bad when she had her "bits and pieces" in it. At least the skylight brightened it up.

"Seeing the sky gives you hope."

Poor Ag.

"Is life generally without it?" I asked.

She just looked at me with her small, sad face. "What do you think?" she said.

I felt an overwhelming tenderness for her. "Well, Aggie, I hope you've a good time here. I really do. We'll do all we can to help you enjoy it and feel better. I think the first thing to do, though, is stay away from the grog."

Totally the wrong thing to say. She lifted her head and gave me a daggers look.

"You just don't understand, do you? The one thing I really enjoy is a nice drink at the end of the day and you'd grudge me that."

I decided not to argue on her first day, though I confess I did feel like closing the trapdoor on her expensive patent leather shoes. Jack hello'd from below. The Hare Krishna chorus of goat bells, bless their little wet noses, could be heard approaching.

"Better fly and relieve a few engorged teats." I made my way down the ladder.

"Poor dumb animals!" Agatha flung herself on to a pile of straw. "Milk should be fed to their little babies, not used for cooling cups of coffee. Making milking machines out of sensitive creatures!"

"If only I could! My fingers wouldn't be in a permanent state of cramp."

I shut the trapdoor as gently as I could.

"Little sis settled in?" Jack had one and a half goats milked. The nicer one and a half. He kept the dregs for me.

"Anyone home?" His voice went up a notch.

"When you've apologised for leaving the most cantankerous animal to me, I'll be sociable."

He stopped milking in mid-squirt. "Could have sworn there's some sort of kinship with old crabby there."

Very *drôle*. I refused to be drawn.

"Only in her endowments, Jack. Nothing else."

"How stoopid of me, Pips."

And then that laugh that made the goat's ears prick up, the milk suddenly go back up from where it came.

"My abject apols, Pips. I'll do the crabby nanny when I've finished Blackie." He scratched his head and wiped his nose on his sleeve. Just as well the health inspector only visited cows.

"Serio, Philippa, how is the little sis? She nearly drove the taxi guy crazy stopping to pee at every café she took a fancy to. Bad bladder run in the family?"

"Only when the alcohol level needs topping up. Afraid Aggie's problem comes out of a bottle. My suggestion that it might be a good idea if she gave it up met with a poor reception. Still, maybe if she gets looked after here, enjoys the sun and flowers, she'll feel life is worth living."

Jack shook his head.

"You don't think so, Jack?"

"Naw, not in a million years. Had the same problem with a girlfriend, once. Been there before."

Great. Goats *and* Aggie *and* Dorrie and Ast. Life never looked so good.

Chapter Nine

❦

Where late the sweet birds sang

In the event, Dorrie and Ast were delighted with our Ag. They had wonderful moaning sessions together, over our wine, while Jack and I squirted milk into pails, made cheese and butter, the taste of which they complained about but couldn't seem to get enough of. Ag felt she shouldn't really "get close" to the goats as they might go off their milk, missing her when she left. I told her goats didn't have those sorts of finer feelings, that one hand giving carrots and cabbage was as good as another.

"It's really you, Philippa, who has no finer feelings. Animals have their sensitivities, even more than humans."

There was no way to disprove that, except by study and practical observation. And, like all prejudiced people who find excuses for anything, she refused to alter her perceptions for long enough to actually do anything in case reality conflicted with her dearly-held beliefs. Or interfered with her imbibing.

Occasionally, Dorrie strolled out to the dairy to help bring back the freshly-made butter or cheese. Her timing was faultless. And the advice she had to bestow! And for free! "Always better to steam things, never boil," she said. "Boiling wrecks the cells in the plastic tubing. It's OK for stainless steel, like your cutters and things and cheesecloths. Saw a steamer going cheap at De Bruger's farm. They're going back to Holland. They couldn't get their permanent papers. Told they were 'undesirables' – all because they grew a little weed for their own consumption in the polytunnel. You'd think they were selling it to the schoolchildren in Aix."

"You haven't given any to Aggie, I hope," I said.

"Ag knows more about smoking pot than you'd learn in a lifetime."

I detected a distinct smirk behind her words. How come everyone tried their damnedest to get one up on me?

Except Jack. He stretched an arm towards me as Fatso waddled her way back to the den of iniquity cradling milk, butter and cheese.

"We can probably kiss goodbye to the bread too," I said to his pleading, blue eyes.

He had me glued to him in seconds, goat smells notwithstanding. I noticed nothing except softness, tenderness and a slight fullness.

"Don't let them get to you, Pips. We'll do that course in Aix which means we'll be away most of the day. And at weekends we can visit the cabinetmaker in St Paul."

"Great! We live here to get away from it all only to have to rush off into the distance to escape from undesirables."

The *ébéniste* managed to be like the man whose mousetrap was so good people beat a path to his door. Except that Michel Petitpot lived at the top of a cobbled street, too narrow for traffic but perfect for donkeys.

We passed through a dark doorway in a white wall and into an equally dark hallway with a pin-prick of light in the distance.

"*Allez-y!*" he urged to what must have looked like a pair of frightened goms.

He had the sort of face that made me feel I had a previous incarnation in a dark, medieval era swarming with north African types. The way he looked at me didn't dispel my crazy notion. It was as if he knew me. From the inside.

His dark skin glistened with sweat; large, dark eyes stared through curls tumbling onto his forehead. He smelt of sawdust and lavender. His hand stretched towards me, hesitated and then firmly grasped my shoulder to usher me away from darkness.

"*Michel? C'est toi?*" a female voice somewhere in the distance asked.

"*J'arrive,*" he answered, his voice on the verge of gruffness, or a sore throat.

A child sat in the middle of the floor playing with

sawdust. A tiny speck in the middle of what looked like an enormous greenhouse. Plants festooned the windows on two sides, some of which bore fruit.

"Say!" Jack gushed. "Tomatoes!"

"*Et melons*," the carpenter added, pointing to a huge plant with nets supporting the melons.

"I see they've got their brazeers." Poor Jack attempted levity but Michel Petitpot stared at me for an explanation.

I giggled instead. Of course, every Frenchman is an egomaniac – he thought I was laughing at him.

I straightened my face, excused my behaviour, tried to explain and stop the red from spreading everywhere. He was not amused. Sex and its accoutrements are a serious matter to the French. Enjoyable, but serious.

Madame Littlepot whisked the child into her arms and took off through the glass doors.

Silently, Monsieur l'Ébeniste took a length of wood, smelt it, rubbed a hand along it, bent it and finally hit it with a hammer.

"For a test," he explained.

It was "*juste à point*", like a well-roasted fowl.

"Don't much like the colour," I whispered to Jack.

"I'd keep quiet about that," he said as he tapped the side of his nose.

Within two hours we had the makings of a substantial cupboard, albeit in jigsaw pieces spread over the floor. We had lost ourselves in its construction, mere ants ferrying bits of wood here, cut-outs there. Something like camaraderie was in the air, soundlessly bonding us as we moved silently about the room. At one stage I bumped into Michel, clung there, seagull to cliff, then back to *terra firma*.

When coffee time came with the return of Madame and offspring, we reluctantly gathered around the steaming mugs and *gaufrettes*.

Michel and Jack chatted easily, brother to brother. I was left with Madame who either stared at the floor or shovelled bits of biscuit into the child's mouth.

"What age is he?" I tried the well-known path to a mother's heart.

"Just sixteen months." To the point, without a smile.

"Very good-looking. Must take after his mother."

Not a word of a lie. However, I was wasting my time. She stared into space as if I didn't exist.

I gave up. Rubbed my fingers along Jack's neck instead. He pretended not to notice but I knew he'd remember later. Hoped he would.

"For Chrissake, Pipsy," he hissed.

I got up and walked through the French window before I skinned his shin.

The garden *was* a joy. Pinks, mauves and deep reds shimmered in the sun and a row of Robinia cast its lacy shadow. Weathered sculptures, carved from tree-trunks, stood or lay amongst the flowers. A cat lay curled in a mother's outstretched arms, her ribs an empty birdcage. Beyond the row of Robinia a circle of wooden children played ring-a-rosy, the child in the middle crying wooden tears. Here was the real artist, not the one who made shelves and presses for a living.

"Where'd you get to, Pips? Always going off on your own."

A girl knew when she wasn't wanted.

"Not speaking now? Some character, that Michel. Told me his real life was out here, in the open air. But no one would buy them. 'Too full of pains', he said. What ya think?"

He put an arm around me. I melted. Stupidly. A weakling when touched.

"I agree," I said. "See the child with the petrified tear? A girl – the female side of Michel, sneered at, belittled. That's why he's got this macho exterior, hiding that softness, that sensitivity."

"My Gawd! The poor guy. Makes you wanna give him a hug."

"Not something I'd advise, Jack. He's got a man-eating tiger for a stablemate. Didn't you see her yellow eyes?"

"Thought that was just the fags. Come to think of it, her incisors seemed . . . hey! You! Had me there for a while."

The glass room got hotter and hotter. We allowed the sweat to drip from our faces and course down whatever creases and hollows it could find. I let Michel and Jack do the sawing, while I sanded and did a little planing. The tiger had disappeared with the child.

"We've enough wood here for a small press, Pips,"

Jack smiled, as we loaded the bits and pieces into the van. "Just a bit of glue and nails and we're in business."

"Better pay for what we've got, Jack. I've a feeling they're living on fresh air."

The relief on Michel's face proved me right. Next time I'd bring them some butter and cheese.

"What they should do," Jack said on the way back, "is get a goat. Build a little wooden cage for it in the garden like the Africans do, and bring the food to it. Goats are sociable craters. They could have it near the house, chat to it. And then when it had its kid – goat chops. Nothing like a bit of kid meat."

"Lets hope they're not *that* desperate."

Ag actually had food ready when we returned. A *ratatouille* with fresh salad, bread and wine. Life was looking up. She even seemed cheerful.

"Gave my room a thorough clean-out. Put down that rice matting Dorrie got me from the De Brugers – the Dutch people who're being deported. Lots of other things there, if you're interested. A cellar full of wine."

Jack's fork stopped in midair. Only momentarily. He likes his food.

"Maybe we ought to take a look," he said. "Things will go cheap if they have to go. Can't say I'll be sorry to see them off. Sold us that crabby goat."

"I always swore I'd murder whoever did that! Not as if you got her cheap, either."

"She probably had a very traumatic time as a kid."

Ag with her homespun philosophy. "They say it scars for life."

"No doubt," I replied. "That still doesn't give her the right to be nasty to those of us who are good to her. It's as if she enjoys it."

"I wouldn't expect *you* to understand, Philippa."

"Of course not. You have a vested interest."

"And what is *that* supposed to mean?"

Agatha showing all her fangs has to be seen to be believed.

"Now, now, girls. You're only just here, Aggie. Settle down a bit. Pips has the strangest sense of humour – I love it, but it's not everyone's glass of bourbon."

"I really don't need the hype, Jack. I can defend myself perfectly well."

In fact, I was downright mad at him for feeling he'd to put in a good word for me.

Hammering in a few nails suddenly seemed a glorious way to spend a few hours.

"Well, I'll leave you two to enjoy what's left of the evening. I've important things to do with a hammer."

Which, once I'd learnt how to remove my flesh in time as the hammer hit the nail, was quite enjoyable. I'd a shelf put together in less time than it takes to make a good dinner. I wondered why I'd never tried it before. I wondered why the whole world didn't make their own presses.

The next was a little tricky, as the structure had a slight wobble. I needed a third hand to steady it while I fitted the second shelf. Shortly, it was quite clear why people left these things to the experts.

"Jack!"

He came, grinning. Delighted to be needed. Wordlessly, he put the whole thing together in minutes.

He looked to me for a pat, somewhere.

Sour, frustrated and mean, I didn't oblige.

"Don't you love me any more, Pips?"

Did I ever? I doubted whether I liked even myself.

One day melted, literally, into another. The heat sapped my energy before I'd even quit the scratcher. Dragging myself to the milking parlour and then the dairy just about put the tin lid on it, while Jack and Aggie's lunchtime *petit verre* dehydrated and rendered me comatose. I could have refused, of course. But I lived in hope that perhaps it would cheer me up, help take the edge off my anguish.

Aggie began with a "My God, it's *hot*," and then filled the glass so full she'd to slurp at it before it could be moved.

"Ah, that's better. Life has something to offer, after all," she went on, not waiting for a response. A necessary ritual before she felt entitled to her fix.

"Well, Jack," she always addressed Jack whenever she was miffed with me, "I think I'll wend my merry way to Aix this afternoon, see what's afoot. Get some brochures from the university. I may as well pick up a degree while I'm here."

I felt certain that wasn't all she could pick up but stuck my finger in my mouth before I could say it. I *could* restrain myself when I really tried.

"You know, Philippa, we've a standing invite to visit *le Comte*." Jack cast his steely blues in my direction. "Great place he has just outside Aix. Very Gatsbyesque."

"Gatsby was thick," I said, relieved to be able to criticise someone who couldn't take offence. "A truly wonderful book but not the sort of man I'd want to meet. The narrator, now, what's his name . . . Nick, he sounds nice. Introspective. Just my type."

He knew when to keep his mouth shut, in other words.

"Well, of course, if you don't wanna come, I'm sure Ag and I could manage . . ."

"No need for all that martyrdom. I'll screw myself to the sickening pace."

I could have sworn he winked at our Aggie. That just about put the tin lid on it.

"I saw that wink, Jack. Ganging up on me once again, Agatha?

Jack had the grace to look guilty. Aggie merely raised an eyebrow.

"And, Jack, old toot, while we're on the subject of martyrdom, I've decided, finally and after much deliberation, that I've had my fill of matters caprine. Not all those tiny bleats, nudges or pats of cheese have managed to convince me they're fully paid-up members of the human race – and before you rush to their defence, I *know*, up here," I pointed to my grey matter, "that they're not human or even want to be. What I'm trying to say is that I've sought some sort of middle ground, something I can latch on to into the capricious caprine world – and failed. For the simple reason – there is nothing!" I ended my case, exhausted.

"Philippa! I could have sworn you slurred that last bit!" Jack had the cheek to say. "Never mind. You've just had a few scoops too many in this heat. You'll feel all right by nightfall when all the four-leggeds turn in to the parlour."

And he laughed!

"*I'll* help you, Jack," Aggie rushed in to put another nail in rotten old sis's coffin. "Goats are very sensitive. They pick up vibes," she added meaningfully.

It was about time a lock was fitted on the cellar. You never know when a goat might break its neck searching for a little drinky.

That particular afternoon was blissful. Time stretched towards a non-existent full stop at goat-milking time. I had another scoop or three, got down the stack of books I hadn't even touched since my arrival, cut myself some small chunks of real cheese encased in plastic and settled on the couch with the gurgling stream before me and the sun and heat at a safe distance. Never having been a Margaret Atwood fan, I thought of giving her another go. But that could wait. There was that exciting book on symmetry in nature, how everything corresponds to a pattern – except where it doesn't – a world where Fibonacci numbers reign supreme.

After three pages, my brain gave up. It reminded me of that incomprehensible book designed to explain space to the layman, to be followed by another, helping to explain the first. By the time Jack and Aggie had finished squirting milk into pails, making butter, yoghurt and cheese, I was ready for some excitement.

"Jack, I really think we ought to take up *le Comte's* invitation. It would be rude not to. The sooner the better. How about this evening?"

"You can count me out – no pun intended." Ag slid to the couch like a fallen tree.

I didn't dissuade her, offered her a glass of wine and the rest of the cheese.

"Dorrie and Ast said they might drop in," Ag informed us.

That did it.

"Well, Pips, on with the motley, or go as you are. The Count doesn't wait on ceremony. We all meet in *Les Deux*."

"All?" I asked.

"Yep. Usually quite a crowd. Everyone knows about his *soirées*."

Not a word of a lie. The bodies in the café's dark interior spilled on to the chairs outside under the awning. Saturday's party mood was everywhere, the freest day in the week for those who didn't have goats to milk.

Yellow, black and red silk shirts abounded. The women wore white, the colour of money. For white you have to be slim, bronze and wrinkle-free.

159

They greeted each other with a "Lisette" or a "Simone" here and a "Gilles" or "Léon" there, flourishing glasses of *pastis*. Our northern penchant for wine at the drop of a hat is totally *infra dig*. Wine is for food only.

"What'll it be, Pips?

"Wine," I said, never one to follow fashion.

He returned, haloed by the light from the lanterns.

"Bit like old times, eh?" He gave me a peck on the cheek. I felt I'd noticed him for the first time in weeks. I kissed his full, moist lips. And, even more interesting, he responded.

"Love is a many-splendoured thing," a voice droned behind us. We turned to face a tanned face with white hair, slightly forward, though perfect, teeth like Charlton Heston. "Please! Don't permit me to interrupt this . . ." his hand stretched towards us.

We parted instantly. Nothing like an audience to put you off the sensual.

"'And true plain hearts do in the . . .' ah, I forget!" He slapped his forehead a felling blow.

. . . "'faces rest'," Jack finished for him.

"*Merci!*" He clasped Jack's hand. "Marc Montremontant. *Enchanté!*"

We introduced ourselves. A wink from Monsieur Le Comte and the waiter spirited another glass of white wine towards us – the most astonishing wine I'd ever tasted.

"*Spécial*," the Count informed us quietly. He had the appearance of doing everything quietly. "Made from the sun-ripened grapes at my own *propriété*. Only a few thousand bottles. That way the good wine is not diluted, like a woman with too many lovers, eh?"

He looked at me for an answer. All I could do was blush. It seemed to be enough. His pupils dilated. He came towards me and deposited a kiss *à la Bretonne*, his expensive breath all over me. A man who believed he was unfailingly attractive. I edged closer to Jack. I hated to give anyone what they wanted to take without asking.

"*Pardon*, Mademoiselle," Monsieur Le Comte said, manfully hiding his remorse. "My mother, she was a *lady*. Never a cross word. *Toujours la politesse*, even under duress. Her head sailed high, her smile never dimmed."

She sounded either stupid or very boring. However, not to forgive would have been churlish. I smiled. He was rich, after all.

"You 'ave that same look of her, you know," he said, eyes misting.

Just what I've always wanted – to remind someone of Mummy.

"How on earth did you know Philippa so well?" Jack asked.

"You Americans, you think the world is a laughing oyster." He swallowed the last of his wine and nodded for another.

"However, my mood is indulgent, *mes enfants*. We have a *soirée* at the Château at midnight. You are most welcome."

He got up, bowed to us and went towards the bar to greet the *beau monde* draped around it.

"Well, Jack. This is the life. Dublin was never like it. The smells, the wine, the colours, the *tans*!"

"You shock me at times, Philippa. I thought you were this spiritual appreciator of art with the brains of a colossus, striding the narrow academic world with your unique insights into the psyche of the artist."

I looked at him and saw disappointment. Anger built up somewhere around my kneecaps and stopped dead at my throat where a lump stopped me from shouting, "How dare you think badly of me! On *your* terms!"

But all I said, eventually, was, "And what, pray, do you see instead?"

"Someone who's a bit like a magpie – likes the glitter, has to have the trappings."

I waved my hand for another glass of wine and drank half of it quickly. Nerves. I'd almost forgotten I had them.

"If you really must know, Jack, I like both the 'trappings', as *you* call them, and things of deeper significance. One does not preclude the other. After all, the leaves on the tree are the mere trappings of the essential thing, which is the tree: root, trunk and limb. Life has things to offer in all its forms. One manifestation is not necessarily more worthy than another."

He edged closer to me. I saw him raise a hand to put around me. I pulled back. I didn't want him to come near me again. I was too fragile to be dented, without reason, on a mere whim.

"Please forgive me, Pips. I got carried away. Suppose I hated that son-of-a-whatsit making Bambi eyes at you."

I stared straight ahead at a moth flapping about the lantern.

"Another glass of wine?" he asked.

I acquiesced. Cutting off your nose to spite your face was silly, really.

Jack and I spent one of those rare evenings I was to remember with longing and pain forever after. In the "still point of the turning world", Jack's hair glowed in the soft light, his eyes shone as he looked at me. Not since the adoration of my dog as a child had I felt so loved. Eddie's love always had a desperation to it, a demand for its return, a certain defiance. This was purer, based on what *I* was. Which gave me pause for thought. But only pause. I lapped it up.

"Just like old Paree, Pips."

I allowed him to edge closer to me.

"Just what I was thinking. Nothing to come between us, two or four-legged."

"That was a real shocker, Pips, you not liking the poor old nanny-goats. Thought you'd love them."

"I hadn't counted on their cussedness. Just like people – without their endearing qualities, like nice lips, or other . . ."

"I just love it when you talk dirty." And he kissed me, fully, completely, in full public view.

He came up for air. "I'd nearly forgotten why we're here in the first place. All the hard work wrecks the hormones."

"Just as well, Jack. I found a hole in my diaphragm."

"I know I'm virile, but surely that sort of damage is next to . . ."

"No, it wasn't you. You're good but not as good as a red-hot needle."

"Pips, is there something I'm missing in all this? You wanting to get pregnant?"

"Last thing on my mind – or anywhere else! Enough little kids about the place to do me a lifetime. I'd suggest sabotage if I didn't sound paranoid. Aggie has these queer notions about natural flows being interrupted."

"You think she did it?"

"Aggie always swore the fish fingers she fed the cat were perfectly all right. But . . . it died. Same with the diaphragm. Misguided but not vicious."

"You're very forgiving. You know, Philippa." He paused. I knew it was going to be serious when he used my full name. "You're the best thing ever happened to me – apart from being born, that is. Never felt every cell in my puny body so alive since we met. Life through your eyes is so beautiful to see."

I was fairly bowled over. What's a little hole in a diaphragm compared to such adulation? I'd save the really bad news for when he asked me to marry him.

Without an ounce of moral fibre left in my body, I

allowed the Comte to help me into his jeep and speed us, along with several "beautiful people", towards the Château de Montremontant. We arrived in a fog of wine fumes and bonhomie. Le Comte decanted us at the door, where we were met by three young girls dressed as if they had just descended from the top of a Christmas tree. Their diaphanous gowns revealed all.

"What nipples!" Jack whispered.

"That's not their natural colour. Lipstick."

That fairly floored him. "Well, I never!" he said.

"Gawd, they don't even have knickers!"

"This is France, Jack. They won't get groin rot from the heat."

"I see," he said. Though I felt he didn't, really. Scratch an American and there's a puritan underneath.

We were led through the candlelit hallway into an enormous room with a barrel vault and hundreds of candles lighting up a table that stretched from one end of the room to the other. The fairies helped us to a plate and pointed us in the direction of the delicacies.

"Do not stint yourselves," Monsieur le Comte announced from the doorway, a fairy of about ten on either arm.

Glasses, with champagne bubbling, were brought to us.

"Eat plenty," Jack said after a deep draught of bubbly. "Save us cooking for a week."

Large silver platters were brought through a doorway and placed on the table. With a flourish, a child dressed in military uniform whipped off the lid. I screamed. Several hundred tiny birds, stripped of their feathers and life, nestled on a bed of shredded lettuce.

"Jesus, that's done it!" Jack said, swallowing the last of his bubbly.

I tried to form the words "I'm sorry", but they refused to come. The Count replaced the lid, led me towards the candlelit hallway, opened the door and said, very politely, "Good night, Monsieur, Mademoiselle," bowed and disappeared inside again.

I felt like a dog turd stuck to a shoe.

"Ah, Pips, don't take it so hard," Jack manfully declared. "Those poor birds looked like bits of rubber. And the stink! The goats wouldn't have liked my breath in the morning. Besides, I wasn't *that* hungry."

I tried to put one foot in front of the other.

"Pips! Stop this at once! Don't worry. It was only *food*!"

"Look, Jack, let's be honest. I've spoilt a lovely evening. And we've to walk all the way to Aix."

He took my hand. "We're together, and all right, and that's all that matters. A bird in the hand is worth at least a dozen on the platter!"

And then that laugh. This time, I gave a little chuckle.

An hour later we were back at the *Cours Mirabeau,* even more crowded and more noisy.

"Let's just mosey on home," Jack said. "I've kinda had enough partying for one night."

Not to mention walking. "Amen to that," I said.

Jack's old van seemed like a luxury coach as we rattled our way out of Aix and towards the hills.

However, *chez nous* the night was but a pup. Or several. Music blared from inside the farmhouse while various shapes pranced about outside. The reedy one was Agatha, writhing to the jungle beat, while Dorrie flopped about like a pregnant seal. Ast was performing strange lunging movements, accompanied by loud grunts.

"I'll slip in the window round the back," I whispered.

"I think I'll knock up a shelf or two before I turn in." Jack stopped the van at the side of the yard in the dark shadows. "In their state, they won't notice the noise."

"Don't make it *too* long," I whispered before disappearing.

I stuck a double dose of wax balls in my ear, shoved my head beneath the pillow and barely woke when Jack came in beside me. He snuggled up, his head resting on my back, his legs nestling neatly beneath my thighs.

"OK?" I muttered.

"Just about. The others have collapsed, for the time being. Just to get their strength back. Think I stood on a nail or something. Apart from that, everything's fine. Sleep tight."

The last sleep I was to get for a considerable length of time.

Chapter Ten

❦

"I am ill, Philippa."

Feeling pleased with myself, I had the goats milked, the milk skimmed, the yoghurt fermenting and the cheese dripping before Jack had stirred. I brought him a cup of coffee.

"Just brewed." I wafted it beneath his nose.

He opened one eye. "Thanks, Pips. Feel rotten. Tried to get up when I heard the goats in the yard. Gave up. Foot's a bit sore."

"If you think this will get me back into bed, think again!"

No laugh. Not even a flicker of a smile.

"Jack? You really ill?"

I felt his forehead. Hot. Clammy too.

What on earth to do in this neck of the woods for a doctor?

Dorrie and Ast were slumped together where they'd fallen. White with sleep, Ast made tiny grunting noises.

I shook him. Quick as a flash, he was up and poised in his combat mode.

"No need for that Ast. It's Jack. Something's wrong."

To give him his due, he followed me without a word.

Jack was lying on his back, an arm thrown back.

"Bad colour," Ast said. He felt his pulse and then his forehead. "Bit of a fever."

"He looks even worse. Said he stood on something."

Ast lifted the bedclothes and looked at Jack's foot. There was a discoloured puncture mark on the sole.

"Wound there, all right. Big enough. Could put some comfrey leaves on it, give him feverfew to take down his temperature. Then a mixture of raspberry and deadly nightshade for the poison."

"Poison?"

"Looks to me like a classic case of poisoning. Wound. Fever."

Within the hour, Ast had Jack looking like a stuffed cabbage leaf. Both feet were encased in comfrey leaves – lest the poison travel from one foot to the other. His forehead had a comfrey compress, each eye a slice of cucumber. I wanted to place a crown of mimosa and lavender, Jack's favourite perfumes, but Ast wouldn't hear of it, said they would "conflict", so the vibes wouldn't know whether he was coming or going.

Meanwhile, Dorrie kept up a chant and a "laying on of hands", which meant she tore up and down Jack's feverish body with arms outstretched, hands pulling at invisible forces – invisible to the naked eye, that is, though highly visible to those with the power of "seeing".

So long as they made Jack well, I didn't care. The weird thing is, I really believed they would; until six in the morning, when the sun was already a yellow disk in the sky and Jack seemed infinitely worse, Dorrie and Ast flat out after their exertions.

"Jack," I said into his ear. He moved his lips, those wonderful lips, now dry and cracked.

"Christ, Jack! What the hell will I do?"

Nothing. Just more sweat and now a strange paleness. Almost blue, his freckles standing out like black dots.

I roused Ast.

"Jack's worse! Where on earth is the nearest doctor?"

"Only one who speaks English is in Aix. Opposite the Dauphin fountain, the house with the pillars," he shouted at my back as I took myself off.

As I climbed into the van, I cursed myself for not having gone sooner, for believing for an instant Ast was more than a bag of air, full of crackpot notions.

A white-coated nurse answered the door. Wanted full details before she'd allow me in. Foreigner means junkie to most French people. I tried not to shake.

Docteur Jean-Paul Grillôt said he'd come *"bientôt"*. I agreed to drive him there and back. He was typically Mediterranean French – not bad-looking, if you like a little Spanish blood with your Frenchman, and a smile. It's the lips. Spanish blood makes them pinky-mauve, thick and delineated. The true Frenchman's mouth, while full-lipped, is never vulgar and often hidden beneath a moustache, as a surprise.

Though silent, I could sense his appraisal of my naked flesh barely hidden by the top of my dungarees.

"This your busy day?" I tried to make conversation and help him not to develop a squint.

"One never knows. *Un accouchement*, just finished."

That explained the six-o'clock shadow.

"Boy or girl?"

He rubbed his chin. "*Voyez* – I can't remember! Alive and well, that's what matters. A first baby. The lady was delighted. Monsieur was absent – an agricultural trip to Lyons."

What could be more important!

"You like it here?" I tried to make conversation, my mind on Jack.

"Here, there is the university, where I teach also. I like the mixture. Not too much illness, not too much books."

Jack was propped up on a mound of pillows. Dorrie was running an ice cube along his forehead. Ast was pouring liquid into his mouth from a spoon. They both looked anxious, which made me even more worried.

The doctor opened his case and performed the usual feats with stethoscope, thermometer and fingers on pulse. He frowned.

I looked at him.

"He is very ill," he said. "A hospital emergency."

The words acted like clamps on my chest.

"That's all we need," I heard Dorrie exclaim. That brought me to.

"You and your useless mumbo-jumbo! Fuck off out of here, you fat, useless slob!" I yelled at her.

Jack opened his eyes. "You OK, Pips?"

Why did he always have to show such concern for *me* when he needed it himself?

"Sure, Jack." I sat on the bed. "You just take it easy. We're going to have to get your temperature down, so we're bringing you to hospital."

"Shit!" was all he managed as Dorrie and Ast slunk out the door.

"Excuse me." The doctor looked at me. "We do not need complications with two patients. Perhaps you stay here, take it easy . . ."

"I'm fine," I said. "Just worried. Jack's in such pain!"

Dr Grillôt spent the next half-hour trying to get a hospital to take Jack. We managed a small one on the outskirts of Marseilles, which had originally been a convent but now boasted a state-of-the-art theatre for plastic surgery, with breast implants a speciality. This information from Jean-Paul, who had the honour of being there to attend the first operation of a student who wanted him to hold her hand. He probably got away lightly.

"It doesn't matter what they do with their scalpels, so long as we get there and get Jack's temperature down."

A local ambulance, a station wagon, drove us to St Sepulchre.

"Do we really need the siren?" I asked.

Jean-Paul looked at me and said nothing. The driver probably wanted to get home to his lunch.

The only part of the journey I remembered later was a child standing by the side of the road wearing a blue dress and straw hat. She waved to us. Her goodbye was a prophecy.

The hospital was a blur of white blobs rushing about. One minute Jack was lying beside me and the next he was wheeled off. A mug of coffee was put into my hand and a chair pointed out to me. It seemed like hours before anyone remembered I was there. Jean-Paul came towards me. He wasn't smiling any more.

"How is he?" I asked.

That shrug.

"Is that all you can say?"

"The antibiotics aren't working very well."

"Have you tried something else? Some people respond differently."

"There is no response."

"Don't be so defeatist. He's as healthy as a trout, give him something else."

"We are doing our best. But in these things, it's a matter of luck."

"Luck? We're talking about getting someone's temperature down. That's a matter of expertise."

"A transfusion might be the best thing, but the blood type is complicated."

"Everything seems complicated in this god-forsaken country! What exactly do you mean?"

"It's a rare blood type he has. Very rare. There are no supplies down here."

"Well, we can get some in Paris. Surely they have supplies there."

"I'll try."

He gave another of those maddening Gallic shrugs.

"The other thing is," I said, "Jack's cousin, Sophie, lives in Paris. Maybe she's got the same blood type."

"A possibility. Who knows?"

"Well, bloody well find out!"

He looked at the floor, looked at me and gave another shrug.

"Very well. I will arrange the hospital in Paris. Get the ambulance ready. But . . . *enfin?*"

"We're expecting a baby!" I yelled.

He looked at me in disbelief. *"Mon Dieu!"* he said. He twiddled with a piece of hair at his temple. "Some things are more important than good facilities. There is love, and kindness too."

"First, we get his temperature down."

He brought me to a bright room on the ground floor. A glass door opened on to a patio filled with flowers. Sitting at a table was a nun, her head bowed, mumbling a rosary. In a corner, Jack lay white and very still. I ran to him.

"Jack? Can you hear me?"

A slight flutter of his eyelids. Jean-Paul put a hand on my shoulder.

"What on earth is going on?" I asked.

He shrugged. "He's still there. Perhaps it will work out. He's young, healthy. But the blood is poisoned – a septicaemia of some virulence."

"We'd better get him to Paris. You arrange the hospital."

"If you insist," he said.

I phoned Sophie. "Delighted" to hear from me and, of course, would do all she could to help. She wrote down the name of the hospital and promised to be there, waiting, blood type test completed, veins at the ready, if need be.

I joined Jack, held his hand as they slid him back into the station wagon.

"Jack," I whispered right into his ear, "Jack, we're taking you to Paris to get some blood. Sophie may well have the same type as you. If not, we've a better chance to get someone else's. Of course, you wouldn't just have any old ordinary blood whizzing in your veins like the rest of us, it had to be different. Typical. Once you get this stuff inside you, free from poison, then the antibiotics will work a bit faster and you'll be right as rain, in time to help with the goats in the morning! I knew it! All this is just an elaborate trick to get a holiday. Well, when you're better, I promise we'll take off to the hills for a few nights camping – let Dorrie and Ast earn their keep for a change and milk the goats."

I could have sworn his lips moved, his eyelids fluttered.

Louise Couper

Within the hour we were heading down the motorway, Jean-Paul and I in the back with Jack.

The ambulance driver wanted to stop for coffee in Dijon. I gave him one of my withering looks; he mopped his brow and carried on. It was almost night when we reached Ste Quentin, the largest hospital in Paris, on the outskirts of the city.

Sophie was at the door to meet us. She rushed to Jack's side and whimpered when she saw him.

"Yes, our blood is the same," she said. "But, Jacques, he looks so *ill*."

Jack was wheeled past us into the hospital. Jean-Paul looked grim. His jaw tight.

"Do you have to look so, so defeated?" I asked.

He shrugged.

Much to Sophie's relief, the hospital had its own stock of Jack's blood type.

"I would have done it for him, but when you don't have to . . . that is even better."

"I'm going in with Jack to make sure they're up to scratch. This Jean-Paul fellow doesn't have any sense of urgency. He's wedded to fatalism."

"It is a national failing. You see our government. *Eh bien*, what can one do?"

We trotted alongside the trolley, into a stainless-steel lift and arrived at the sixth floor.

A white-coated doctor lifted his head, took off his specs and came towards us.

"This is Jack," I said before Jean-Paul plodded his

weary way through the story. "He needs a transfusion now!"

He put on his specs and peered at Jack. "How long?"

"Over twenty-four hours," Jean-Paul got in before me.

Yes, too long and my own stupid fault. I should have got a doctor immediately; I should never have paid attention to those two lunatics.

When they rigged Jack up to a life-support machine, I snapped. "What is that for? Get that blood into him."

Big specs looked at me. Jean-Paul looked at the floor. The machine barely blipped.

Sophie let out a little shriek. My legs went to rubber and my eyes wouldn't focus.

"Jack! You can't just die! Think of the baby! She's to come in the spring with the primroses – that would be a nice name, wouldn't it? Or maybe bluebell? How about Bluebell O'Connor?"

Someone put their arms around me. The room was still. The machine just buzzed.

"Christ! Get the resuscitation thing in here! Don't you see, he can't breathe. You've got to help him!"

They just stood around looking at the floor. Sophie was snivelling into a hankie. Always the hysterical type.

Big specs came towards me, did something sharp to my arm and the room went black.

I opened my eyes to a white ceiling and a white coat.

"*Ça va?*" a white coat asked.

Sophie was at the bedside, her nose was bright red. Her eyes dead. Though she looked pleased to see me.

"Philippa? You awake?"

In a shaft of sunlight stood Jean-Paul, one hand in his pocket, the other on his hip. He was looking out the window.

Then I knew. He was dead. Jack was dead.

"You let him die!" I shouted at Jean-Paul. He didn't budge. The nurse told me to take it easy. Sophie came towards me and held my hand.

"It was over before he left Provence."

That didn't help a bit, not one bit.

I thought of all the things I'd wanted to tell him, how much I loved him, that we would have a baby, what its name would be, who it would look like. But that was not to be. And then I thought of him, his life over just as it had barely begun, his strength in getting the farm, milking the goats, pruning vines, sowing vegetables, doing the backbreaking watering of the tiny plants he would never see grow. I felt his love for me – such a miracle in my life, so unlooked-for, resisted for so long, never fully embraced, never fully returned. Why does it take death to teach us the value of life?

Jean-Paul came towards me. "I think you have had enough suffering for now. You must think of the baby."

Its future blighted already. Its father dead.

"Come, let me help you up, we will get some coffee."

I couldn't drink it. It smelt foul, tasted like goat droppings.

Jean-Paul broke off a piece of *brioche*. "Try, just a little." He held it towards me.

For him, I took it. And then immediately felt guilty for bothering to care about his feelings when Jack . . .

"Some advice, from my course on psychiatry – don't be too harsh with yourself. Take care of you, inside. Remember the baby."

I hadn't forgotten. The baby was still alive, at least.

I sipped the coffee, tried to swallow the *brioche*.

Jean-Paul lifted my hand to his lips. I pulled it back.

"Sorry, Philippa. Just a friendly gesture. I have a wife and baby that I love very much. I'm not looking for love, but I've plenty to give, if you need it."

That fairly pole-axed me. "I suppose I need it all right. Just confused. Numb. Jack was with me last night. Now he'll never be with me again. That's . . . impossible . . ."

"I know. I wasn't underestimating your problem."

"Underestimating your problem"? I hated it when people clothed feelings in mechanical words. He was obviously watching too much Sky news.

"What I mean, Philippa, is I know Jack meant a lot to you. His death is hard."

That was better. I was beginning to warm to the silly twit.

"The baby, you must think of the baby," he said, taking my hand. I let him.

"*Voilà!*"

Sophie.

"Cremation or – the other?" she asked earnestly.

"Actually, I hadn't thought quite that far . . ."

I saw Jean-Paul put a finger to his lips, which Sophie ignored.

"But you must think about it. Jack would have wanted ashes – scattered over the Bois de Boulogne. It became very special for him. We spent a lot of time together there."

That was *one* place they certainly would not fertilise.

"He's to be buried in Aigue, the place he loved," I said firmly.

Also, I wanted a body to visit, to cry over.

She sloped off to persecute someone else.

"Listen, Philippa," Jean-Paul said, "I will arrange for the body, for Jack, to be sent to Aigue. I know the priest there, a friend of the family. He will arrange for it to lie in the church. Perhaps it could all be finished in a day or so."

Finished? Did something like this ever finish?

"OK. That sounds OK," I said. I sipped the coffee. Socks. Dirty ones.

"But before . . . if you would like to say a last 'good-bye', we can go now to the mortuary."

"Do we have to?"

"It is a good idea, I think," he said.

"I couldn't. It sounds too . . ." I made tiny flowers from a tissue and let them drop to the floor.

"We'll take it slowly."

Except that once we'd arrived there, I didn't want to go in. Going in, seeing. Reality.

"It is important," Jean-Paul whispered. He put an arm around my shoulder. "You must, Philippa."

"But I've no hankie," I said.

He produced a large white one.

A nun sat at the entrance. She opened the door. "Welcome to the house of the dead," she said.

Jean-Paul led me inside. "Look," he said.

I wanted to keep my head down, count the tiles on the floor, go back and chat to the nun. Anything but . . .

Jean-Paul gently lifted my chin. We walked towards a bed covered in a sheet. And there . . .

"Oh, God! No! Please, Jack. Not you . . ."

I felt a band of iron around my throat.

"Breathe!" Jean-Paul held my hand.

I tried. And let out a long, low noise.

"That's it, breathe again."

"Oh, Jack! He's really dead?" I looked at Jean-Paul.

Jean-Paul nodded. "Just take your time, say good-bye."

How could I? How to say good-bye to a life?

I lifted Jack's hand. Ice-cold. Put my hand on his beautiful red hair. Damp. His face carved in marble.

"Jack. Oh, God, Jack! I wish I were there with you. It's not fair that I should live and you . . . lie there."

Jean-Paul brought chairs and we sat down.

I lifted Jack's hand again. Kissed it. Held it against my cheek. "I'm so sorry, Jack, for not getting the doctor sooner, for not being nicer, for hating the goats, for criticising the butter and cheese. I'd eat tons of it, if only you'd come back to me, just so I can tell you how much I . . ."

But he never would.

Beside me Jean-Paul made a noise, a low, whimpering noise. He had a hankie to his face. I put my hand on his arm. We fell against each other.

Slowly, I got up, kissed my lovely Jack on the cheek and pulled the sheet over his face. "Goodbye, my love. Goodbye."

&

Somehow, I managed to accompany Jack back to Provence, to the hills he loved. His body held no terrors for me now. It was no longer Jack but the shell in which he carried himself about. Yet it was comforting to be with it. To reassure myself that this was not him and to know that part of him was still alive, inside me. I put my hand on my baby. "It'll be OK, you, me, the goats. Maybe Jean-Paul and his wife will help us. We'll get rid of Dorrie and Ast, invite Michel Petitpot over. You'll be able to play with his little boy."

The priest was already at the church, to greet the coffin. He had a place prepared for it, surrounded by candles. Someone played the organ.

"Tomorrow," he bent towards me, "if you would like music for *l'enterrement*, you may choose from two hymns. The organist charges F100."

I couldn't have cared less.

"*Eh bien*, he has a wife and five children to feed!"

Lucky him, he'd always have someone.

There wasn't a single light on at home. Dorrie and Ast had quit the pantry when Jack's generosity could no longer be counted upon. But where was Aggie?

I managed to milk three goats with engorged teats, put the milk in the settling pan and bring in the cottage cheese from yesterday. It seemed a lifetime away. The world had done an about-turn. I couldn't face making butter – I'd always hated it, anyway.

Just as I was gathering the various cloths to bring home and wash, there was a crash overhead. It had to be . . .

"That you, Aggie?" I shouted. A bang and a noise like hard shelled peas pouring from a sack.

I climbed the stepladder. It *was* peas pouring from a sack.

"Mouse!" screeched Aggie. If there'd been a chandelier, she'd have hung from it. As it was, she was practically glued to the roof trusses.

"Get down, Agatha! If it's a mouse, it won't be interested in you. It prefers peas."

"I tried to kill it but just missed."

"You're bloody lucky the floorboards haven't snapped. Talk about using a sledgehammer to crack a nut!"

I retrieved the wooden coatrack Michel gave us on our last visit.

"I presume the worst has happened." Aggie, her usual sympathetic self.

I said nothing.

"How does that leave us? Have you any title to the place? You *were* his common-law wife, after all. French law recognises that."

Did I brain her now or give her the wine to do it herself?

"Pity you hadn't children – that would have cemented it. Still, I suppose we can stay on for now. Do we have to milk those poor animals?"

"Seeing you love them so much, I'm sure you'll be the first to wish to relieve them of their engorged teats."

Like all self-styled animal lovers, she didn't want to do anything practical. Animals were cuddly toys with brains.

"Yoo, hoo!" A voice from the yard.

Dorrie and Skinnymalink! "Tell them to crawl back into whatever hole they came from. I never want to see them again."

"Not even Jack's death has any effect on you!" she said, slamming the trapdoor.

If only it were true. If only . . . There were so many "if onlys". If only we'd never done that stupid woodwork course, had nails lying around the place. If only I'd never met Jack . . . If only I hadn't gone near the Louvre that morning and let him find me there . . . If only I had stayed, discontented, at college and measured out my life in articles on art, bowls of rice with kombu seaweed . . . kismet, Jack. Kismet.

Chapter Eleven

❧

And all men kill the thing they love

A noise in the yard startled the hens.

"A car," Aggie said. "Two men."

"Probably to do with Jack's funeral. I'd better go."

I dragged myself towards them.

"Mademoiselle Philippa Woodcock?" the one with wiry, black hair asked in almost perfect English.

I nodded.

He took what seemed like an ID card from his pocket.

"*Police Judiciare*," he announced. "Inspector Chambertain," he pointed to his companion. "Lucas. May we have several words with you?"

What could I say – "No"?

Aggie looked a little startled. "Don't worry, Ag, it's probably some formality about the burial. They've queer procedures in Provence."

"I'll go and put the kettle on." She disappeared into

the kitchen. I pointed to a couch and chair. They refused both. I felt a slight ripple of tension.

The wiry-haired one played with his ID card, bending it, flicking it with a finger.

"We have had a report from a source. It seems the death of Monsieur Jack O'Connor is not so straightforward. Some questions to be answered."

I was the one to sit down first. I wanted to yell at him to get the hell on with it, stop fiddling with his bloody ID card.

"When did Monsieur Jack?" he enunciated every vowel and consonant, "begin to feel – unwell?"

"Well, it was, I suppose it was the next day, really, that I noticed anything. He'd said he'd pricked his foot. He became really ill, shaking. I called the doctor, who'll probably tell you in more detail what . . . what he died from."

"Yes, yes," he said impatiently, his card bent in two. "We have spoken to the doctor. We want your version of events."

"My version of events?" I screamed at them. "Jack died. That is the only version. He became sick and died. Now just – go."

The quiet one came towards me, looking bigger now, almost menacing.

"We are examining . . . we have certain information that you intended some harm to your, em, *bon ami*."

My brain flicked through my database of anyone who could suggest such a thing. Aggie? Unlikely. Dorrie? A distinct possibility.

I decided it was now a question of survival.

"Where did you get such information? What sort of *evidence* do you have for such a suggestion?"

They were now *tête-à-tête*, arms waving, mouths going nineteen to the dozen.

Aggie came in with the tea and coffee. White-faced. No wonder. She'd regret the day she encouraged those two layabouts to invade our farm.

"It looks like," I said as menacingly as possible for a truly gentle person, "someone's sold me down the Swanee, insinuating I *murdered* Jack. Where on earth do you think they got that idea?"

She looked genuinely startled. And afraid. She read the signals perfectly.

"Don't look at me like that! I know Dorrie was mad when I told her you didn't want to see her again, but doing something like this?"

She faced the inquisitors.

"Look here, you two! Philippa has her faults – I'd be the first to admit that – but she loved Jack, really loved him."

I could have sworn there were tears in our Ag's eyes.

The two guardians of the peace rounded on me.

"All the same, we have to bring you to the office for questioning. Some loose ends?"

And so it was that I was led away, not quite in handcuffs, though without the freedom to refuse. For killing my best friend, the first person I'd ever fallen in love with, the only person who could give me three orgasms where before there had been merely one. Nothing would ever be the same again.

They grilled me for hours. One who looked like an ape, but acted like a kindly grandfather: another who was handsome, intelligent and quite brutal.

I tried freaking out, the screaming job with my hair all over the place and saliva dribbling down my chin. They just sent in a police lady to mop me up and tie back my hair. I tried the wise, intelligent genius I was supposed to be. They twisted everything I said so that I began to say the opposite to what I'd meant. It was dawn before they let up. I was brought to a dark, smelly cell with an aluminium bucket for a loo. The door was very firmly shut behind me.

I lay on the bed and cried. And cried. For me, for Jack, for the goats, even Aggie got a slight mention. When the tears dried up, I examined the room for a suitable weapon of death. The handle of the bucket: perhaps I could lodge my head between it and the bucket? A bit slow. The foot of the bed on top of my throat? Maybe it would only crush the voice-box. The window was barred, the sink was as tiny as a birdbath. I fell asleep, having exhausted all possibilities.

Two minutes later there was clattering and shouting at the door. The key turned in the lock.

"Thank God! She's alive!"

Ag. Perhaps I was having a nightmare.

"What have they done to you? Look for cigarette burns beneath the clothes, Eddie."

Eddie?

"I won't say 'I told you so', Pips – but . . ."

"Eddie, please, for once, just say nothing." It was then I realised what it was about Eddie that had always hovered on the edge of consciousness, that part of him I couldn't abide. His damn chat, at times when you want to hear the silence, times when you want to sort something out, when you want to just be.

And then I saw his crestfallen face. How could I be such a bitch? But this time, I wasn't caving in. It was time to insist.

My life was on the line.

"They think I killed Jack."

They looked at each other, and then at me.

"I know you're capable of almost *anything*, Philippa, but . . . you're my sister."

"That doesn't make me any the less a murderer." Perhaps even more so?

"You know what I mean! We've had our differences, but *murder*? Never."

I didn't like to spoil her illusions. I lay back on the bed. It stank of stale piss and vomit, French style. Infinitely worse. So, this is it, I thought. I'd descended into the pit of the world. They talk about "rock bottom", but it's nothing like as solid. It's soft and stinking, no footholds, nothing to climb but slime.

"She's gone into one of her stoons, Eddie," Aggie whispered, thinking I wasn't listening. I heard the superior tone, all right; trying to pretend she was saner

than I. Well, she was welcome to him. Eddie after Jack
would be dried bread after honey cake.

They left, eventually. I didn't care that they'd left me
in this stinking hell-hole. It was appropriate. Life
without Jack was shit.

The men in suits came back. This time they
brought a pinstripe with them, a Commissaire d'Orée.
Complexion of summer holidays on the Côte; smell of
expensive restaurants and even more expensive
cologne. Just my type. I almost warmed to the occasion.
I was ordered to follow him, along a corridor, into a lift
and up a short flight of stairs.

"*Eh bien*, tell *me* all about it," he said when we had
seated ourselves in his room – a room that looked like
someone's sitting-room, Provencal cottons and dried
flowers. Probably reserved for the truly murderous to
give them a sense of normality.

"'It'?" I asked.

"The death of Jack."

I don't know whether it was the smell of his
perfume, the way his hair took a slight turn at the
temple and showed a few grey hairs, or the way his
mouth settled: creased and moist – whatever it was, I
caved in and blubbed.

"We'd just come back from a sort of party at the
Château. We'd two hangers-on eating us out of house
and home and, as I'd had a rather traumatic evening
with a dish of dead birds, I left them to it and went

straight to bed. Jack decided to stay up and put up some more shelves. I remember him coming to bed."

The last time he snuggled up to me.

"He said something about hurting his foot but that he was OK."

I hadn't even bothered to wake up.

"So, next morning, he was worse. In agony. A high temperature, sweat pouring from him."

The pinstripe nodded.

"Dorrie and Ast said he'd be fine, they'd get his temperature down. Stupidly, I listened to them. They did some mumbo-jumbo over him, tied his feet up in comfrey leaves, brewed up some herbs."

He moistened his lips.

"I'd have believed anything, I suppose. I just didn't realise how serious it was. I thought he'd been overdoing it in the fields – we'd been planting vegetables that week. Trying to turn vegetarian. So, at first, I didn't pay much attention."

The Commissaire had a button undone on his shirt, just where his floating ribs should be.

"Then, later, Jack began to pour sweat – not the kind you'd see at the bottom of a ski slope when the sun was shining and you'd overexerted yourself. It was *sinistre*."

I wanted to scream, to tear the room apart.

I stood up instead. Unsteadily.

D'Orée held out a steadying hand, nodded sympathetically, again moistened his lips. How could I feel any man attractive when Jack was dead? Probably because I was human, after all.

"Did something like that ever happen to you?" I asked him.

"A long time ago," he said. "There was someone. In Africa. She caught malaria – wouldn't use insect repellent. Said it gave her a headache."

He moistened those lips again. "*Finalement*, a headache wasn't the worse thing. She died."

We looked at each other.

I was released into a bright, dry afternoon, filthy clothes, hair and skin. I shuddered to think what prisoners endured.

Ag was there, funereal garb and mien.

"Just been on the phone to Professor Goodbody. Told him about your ordeal," she said.

"You what!" I shrieked.

"No need for those histrionics. He's coming over to help you. He said he perfectly understood how you felt, as he'd been through it all with Matilda, but that at least you had a body!"

"We may very well be able to provide him with one. You always said how well you looked in white!"

Tears shot down her cheeks. If the anger doesn't work, try the waterworks.

"I was only doing my best. You're so mean and awful. And I didn't even mention the baby!"

"The baby! I should bloody well hope not! The

baby has nothing to do with you or anyone else. It is part of *me*, not a subject for gossip."

I suddenly realised I was wasting my breath, that my baby needed peace and quiet. Worst of all, no one understood, really understood, how I felt. Laughter finds a companion but everyone runs a mile from sorrow, the dark shadow. I needed to find a hole to crawl into.

❧

There was to be no resting-place. We arrived at the farmhouse to find it had been invaded by those I thought I'd given the slip for good – not only Bonkers, but Henry and Constantia, piranha teeth herself. They'd wasted no time in making themselves at home.

"Philippa," she gushed, blinding me with her fangs. "Let me get you a *tasse de café*."

"It will only keep me awake, thank you," I replied.

"Glass of Pernod? Wine?" Henry invited.

Not if it came from a crystal goblet.

"Oh, that *would* be nice," Agatha, oh treacherous sister, simpered.

"Just give them to her one at a time," I said firmly to Henry's back.

Piranha teeth curled her lip but pretended we were the best of friends. That psychology course I did on body language has a lot to answer for – it forces you to understand, and therefore to *forgive*.

Once Henry brought the drinks and a "little something" he had concocted in the kitchen, Bonkers arrived with the aroma.

"Well, Dean Woodhouse, don't know whether this is *chien* or *chat*," he said, emphasising the "t", "but jolly good it is, too."

Since fingers were made long before forks, he ladled the rice, embedded with bits of black, into his enormous, plastic-filled mouth.

"Well, I must confess, Professor, I haven't seen the cat for days!" I said, somewhat hysterically.

Piranha teeth put down her plate. One so delicate and dainty had to be careful in foreign parts.

Bonkers was impervious, sharing the Pernod with Aggie.

"Thirsty weather," he said, scarcely pausing for breath. "Big day ahead of you tomorrow, Woody. You'll need your strength. Funerals are pretty dismal affairs, though Tilly never had a proper one. I've a sneaky feeling she'll come swimming back one day – she has to. I miss her too much."

By sunset I wanted to die, to follow Jack wherever he was, I wasn't fussy. Staying around with the motley crew didn't seem any sort of fair exchange. Why had you to die, Jack? Was it really all my fault? Why on earth did I ever meet you in the first place?

I was groping for answers when a figure hove into view. Commissaire d'Orée. He said nothing, just stood there. A change from the platitudes that circled the air all day. I got up, invited him out to the farmyard. The goats trotted towards us. I looked at the Commissaire.

"I was born on a farm." He shrugged.

They followed us into the milking parlour where, like an expert, the Commissaire removed his jacket, sat on the stool and began squirting milk into the bucket.

"It took me a month of Sundays to get that bloody goat to even stand for me, let alone milk her," I said.

He turned his head, while still keeping it against Whitie's flank.

"Ah, *chère* Philippa, you don't realise French nanny-goats prefer Christian Dior to Yardley."

"I knew I'd been doing something wrong."

I watched the froth rise, bubble and disappear. Just like Jack. And life. Out, brief candle.

I put my arm on his shoulder. Two squirts. Then one. He turned towards me. I fell on to his shoulder.

Who knows where comfort ends and sex begins? I'm not talking about love, though sympathy and love are not unrelated. I mean the comfort of arms about you, the feel of flesh against yours.

He patted my back, made soothing French noises. And suddenly let go of me.

I raised an eyebrow. He ran his hand through his moist hair, flicked away the drips of sweat from his forehead.

"I have a good wife and a beautiful daughter," he said. He lifted my chin, kissed my lips. "You are truly beautiful, inside and out."

Fool that I might be, I liked him even better. Restraint is rare.

"Don't worry," I said. "I understand. They're both lucky to have you – and I didn't really need . . . you know, *everything*, to feel better. The 'everything' was my gift to you. My thanks."

He swallowed hard, and stood up. I watched as the dust settled on the road long after his car had disappeared down the track.

What was left of Jack was lowered into a deep hole of red clay on a sunny morning. Sophie swore Jack wouldn't mind being buried in a Catholic graveyard.

"He always said 'once you're gone, you're gone'," she said. I envied her knowledge of him, put my hand on our baby. At least I had that.

The priest blessed the grave, shook my hand and then disappeared. Bonkers and Aggie clutched each other, united in their hangovers. Piranha and Henry wandered off, arms entwined, without a care for Henry's helpless twins, needing their father.

And no one there for me.

Jean-Paul Grillôt had invited everyone to a funeral breakfast. I declined.

"You'd be better off with people," he said.

"Not this lot. There are worse things than being on your own."

He dropped me at the farm. I'd left the van to Aggie in the vain hope that she wouldn't drink too much, seeing she'd be driving.

In the late morning sun, the farm glowed on the hillside, a thing apart, something that would endure when all of us had gone.

"*Au revoir*," Jean-Paul hugged me goodbye.

"*Au revoir*, Jean-Paul, and – thanks."

The hens ran to greet me. "What on earth will I do with you lot?"

Inside, the house seemed to hold its breath, waiting. I poured a glass of *rosé*. One sip was enough. Pointless without company. In the bedroom, the bed had been stripped to the mattress, the windows left open.

"Who the fuck had the cheek to do this!" I yelled. I wanted to feel Jack's shape on the sheets one more time, smell his body. Everything had been tidied. Put away. As if it had never happened.

I pulled open the wardrobe. At least they were all there. Jack's clothes. His working shoes. I lifted them. Still muddy. I put my hand inside. The shape of his toes was still there. That was something. I pressed a finger into each one.

"Your poor, poor toes, Jack. All the hard work, all that water you carried, the plants you grew."

Is anything worth doing if we can be snatched into nothingness in an instant?

Before I knew I'd made a decision, I had my bags packed. And Jack's – to give to Sophie and her boyfriend, to rescue what they wished. I kept the muslin shirt, the one I embroidered with a "J", the one that had the wine stains, the one that smelt of Jack.

Jean-Paul explained that the farm would be sold according to the rules, in true French style. And I knew that French lawyers would see to it that if I was due to get anything, get it I would.

I told Aggie I was leaving.

"You're not just . . . going!" Agatha screeched.

"Definitely. You're always at pains to tell me what a wonderful hostess you are. Well, here's your big chance. I didn't invite any of these people. In fact, it was partly to get away from them that I came here in the first place."

"You still owe them civility, at least!"

"Don't *you* talk to me about civility! You, who gets maggoty drunk at every available opportunity and then has the cheek to rubbish me!"

"I only ever have one or two to cheer myself up. I never had your luck, after all."

"You sound like something out of Hardy, with the fates conspiring against you! Another cop-out, Aggie. You have control over your destiny in the same way I have. The only difference is that you prefer not to acknowledge that. It's so much easier for you to sit, do nothing and complain about the ill turn life has done you."

I stubbed my toe on the piece of timber Jack had left in the hallway. I could hear him say, "Pips, cool it. You'll get your blood pressure up."

He was right. From now on it would be *sauve qui peut*. Nobody gives one tuppenny damn about you. You've to go it alone, sink or swim. The rest of my life had to be lived somehow. I decided to live it the way *I* wished.

Chapter Twelve

❧

Hush-a-bye baby, never said a word

"Leave your good job altogether and you a big noise?" Nellie almost burnt herself with the teapot when I told her of my plan to leave the hallowed precincts of academe for good. "It's not the whole world and his wife that gets made into a dean. You always were clever, but lately you've been acting cracked, what with milking goats and making cheese in the south of France. Maybe you should takes things easy, give yourself a chance to get over your American friend's death. That's what's unsettling you, if you ask me."

"I suppose I'd be still with Jack, toiling away in the vineyard if . . ."

"It's all a lot too soon. Where's it going to end?" Nellie squeaked, spilling tea on her good lace tablecloth. I got up to get a cloth.

"No, don't use hot water. Cold for tea. Did you learn nothing from me?"

"You taught me one important thing, Nellie. How to love."

She smiled to herself.

"Don't know if I did that. Just kindness. In the end, that's what love is. Maybe a bit more, when things get hard. Like this news of yours!"

"Look, Nellie, it makes sense if you see it from where I'm sitting. I was thoroughly fed up when I came back after the summer holidays. There was something wholesome and right about being free of college politics, just doing my research, enjoying it sort of face-to-face without having to go to meetings or meet students who'd mostly prefer to be somewhere else."

I dabbed at the spilled tea while Nellie lifted the cloth.

"What would you live on, Pippy? Growing veg and keeping a cow is all very well. But there's things you'll need to pay for – like electricity and a phone, maybe a car."

I went to the sink to get fresh water.

"Just leave it," she said. "Never liked that tablecloth anyway. The tea stain will remind me of you."

Nellie had a way of saying the simplest thing and making you feel wonderful.

"For what my advice is worth, Little Apples, give it a bit more time. Have a look around. You look worn out by all this business, hot sun and queer French food."

"I've a confession to make. I'm expecting Jack's baby."

She just stared. Gobsmacked.

"So that's what it takes to leave you speechless,

Nellie. Don't worry. We'll be fine. I'll get a nice little place for baby and me. Maybe you'd come and visit us, bounce baby on your knee, teach her nursery rhymes like you did me and Ag."

Nellie mechanically lifted the dishes from the table and, zombie-like, brought them to the sink. She then made the sign of the cross, a prayer for my sinful soul.

"Don't worry, Nellie. I'm going on a retreat – to find out what life is about, why we die."

Nellie turned. "We die because our souls are as black as the ace of spades. But we can save ourselves, there is *eternal* life. A retreat is exactly what you need."

I hadn't the heart to tell her it was a Buddhist retreat, nothing to do with Jesus and crucifixions.

The "retreat house" perched on a spur of the Dingle Peninsula, high above the Atlantic, white against the grey cliffs. A "place of comfort", the brochure said, where you were at liberty to gather whatever wits you felt you had left after the world had done its worst. Just what I needed: peace for my baby and me.

However, I had to find it first.

"Is this the way to the Buddhist retreat house?" I asked an oriental gentleman as I scrabbled my way along a dirt-track with seagulls screaming over my head and mist falling wetly on my face.

"Ten minutes more." He smiled. His toes were muddy and blue with cold but his face looked completely happy. Perhaps if I got a pair of sandals . . .

Over a rise, a white building with a spire surrounded by flags looked over the blue-green sea.

Signposts indicated either the "Meditation Room" or the "Sleeping Quarters". Straight ahead was a long, low building with "sign here" on the outside. Inside, a narrow, dark-haired woman who looked meaningful but said little took my money, handed me a key and pointed the way to a wooden chalet.

Another hopeful had got there before me.

"Christ, what a kip," said the sort of man you might see behind the cashier sign at a bank or chewing a mobile phone in Bewley's. I didn't ask the obvious: why are you here?

"I came because there was nowhere else to go," he volunteered. "Girlfriend left me, I was made redundant, the mortgage was due and there wasn't a thing in the fridge."

He seemed to relax then. All had been revealed.

I kept my own trials and tribulations to myself. I'd no desire to relive them, hear the usual platitudes.

He stuck out a shoe. "Lucky enough I'd got some of the gear."

A Jesus boot, a leftover from the halcyon days of flower power, when I too wore a daisy over my ear and hope in my bosom.

However, I turned away. I hated the sight of men's feet.

"Dinner isn't for another awhile," he said. "I pinched a bit of bread to tide me over. Found it in the press there, probably someone else's." He indicated a bank of presses and shelves.

"Don't let it worry you. The owner will get plenty of karma for doing a good turn," I reassured.

"God, one religion calls it stealing and another says it's karma. You wouldn't know where you are."

I could hazard a fair old guess – to do with manure, but I went to my room instead and left bare-toes contemplating his soul.

Something scuttled in the wardrobe. A freshly caught fly buzzed in a cobweb as a long-legged spider spun filaments around it. I lay on the bed and felt the kind of sharp pain which normally announces a period, and decided it was indigestion.

Strange how we think that "getting away from it all" will solve everything. Left on our own, it brings our problems into sharper focus. Would my baby be all right? How could I bring it up without a father?

A single chime sounded near my ear. I woke to pitch darkness, much bustle and the smell of fried onions.

"Good!" a jolly voice said from the other bed. "I was frightened to move in case I disturbed you." She put on the light. "Restless sleep you had." She squinted at me. "Though you don't snore, thank Buddha! That's why I'm here. My husband snores all night long, impervious to shoves, thumps or shouts. If I hadn't run away for a few nights, I'd have throttled him."

She pulled on a jumper. I sat up and searched for my jacket.

The night air was cold and even damper than earlier. We joined the throng spilling from the other chalets and tents and made our way to the Meditation Room. We left our shoes outside and crept in. A Tibetan monk was there before us, smiling like a lunatic, sitting cross-legged in the middle of the floor. I copied the others and grabbed a cushion. A long, plaintive note issued from the monk, a cross between a yodel and a banshee's wail. The lady-of-the-snoring-husband began to giggle and shake. What seemed like hours later, Monkey stopped and smiled in her direction.

"Some of us come here for relief. To laugh is to release. Laugh!" he ordered.

Of course, she stopped. I could have told him it's only fun if you're not supposed to.

The room began to fill. Some brought their own cushions, while several sported small wooden arrangements designed to raise the bum two inches from the floor. Everyone smiled in the same ghastly way as Monkey, as if this was going to be the best fun, ever.

The bell went again. We took up our meditation positions and stared into space.

"Your thoughts are like the clouds – empty," Monkey told us. "Let them pass."

Easier said than done, when smelly feet and noisily breathing folk are all round you.

Eventually I drifted into a state of total oblivion. All I had was my breath and all I felt was peace. As soon as I began to regret that I didn't just sit and stare into space at home, without having to pay for the privilege, I noticed my aching legs and sore bottom.

Someone got up and left the room. Monkey seemed to be asleep.

I could have sworn I smelt food. Another bell. A light went on. The waif-like ticket woman carried in an enormous bowl of lettuce, grated cabbage and carrot.

"Horse food," Bare-toes moaned. She-of-the-snoring-husband did a good imitation of a neigh and giggled.

A tiny monk in a bright red robe carried in a cauldron of something hot. Beans?

She-of-the-snoring-husband pinched her nose. Beans all right.

"For those of you who are not vegetarians, meatball stew will arrive shortly." She said this as if daring us to eat it.

"Of course, Tibetans are great meat-eaters," I said, fairly audibly. "Dogs – and cats, too."

Monkey laughed. "Dogs maybe, if the crop failed. Often rats. But *never* cats! Too hairy!"

I think it was then and there I decided Buddhists were OK. At least they'd a sense of humour. Except I was the only one who laughed. She-of-the-snoring-husband was silent.

The meatball stew arrived, carried lovingly by a tall, slim, dark-skinned monk. His eyes seemed to latch on to mine. I looked to my neighbour to see if they noticed anything. Bare-toes winked. I knew then it wasn't my imagination.

When he'd served everyone two meatballs apiece, he sat beside me and gave me a few extra.

"Mighoal," he said, stretching a hand towards me.

"Philippa," I replied, before popping a meatball into my mouth.

"Yours?" I enquired, pointing to the stew.

"Bits and bits." He performed a mime of stirring, popping on to a pan. "Meat is by Irish beef."

We sat in companionable silence. The thick, rich gravy spread around my mouth like an oral orgasm. The meatballs melted through my teeth in ecstasy. Thank Buddha for food. The one joy we can experience for ourselves alone.

"So," he said, looking at me with limpid eyes. I never really understood what "limpid" meant till then. His eyes were so liquid they could have slipped out of their sockets.

"So," he repeated, "what is your story?"

I lifted a meatball to my mouth, let it hang between my teeth for an instant, dropped it on to my tongue and then softly pressed it, twirling it, sucking at it and finally, reluctantly, swallowing it.

"Well," I said, plate empty, "it's like this. I was in love with two people. Then I was in love with one. That one died and now there is only me. And my baby. I'm here to find out the why and wherefore. Your sales material says, 'All is nothingness, emptiness.' I was wondering why that's so. What's the point of it all?

Why are people such shitheads? When Jack died, a crowd of vultures descended to drink me out of house and home and have a rare old time at my expense. All under the guise of 'friendship'. Is that the way of *all* flesh? Or have I just happened to hit on a bad seam?"

Limpid eyes looked at me. A tear gathered at the corner of one eye and dripped down the edge of his cheek. He speared a meatball and offered it to me.

I opened my mouth. Wide. It was the nicest meatball I'd ever tasted.

I offered to help him carry his dishes back to the kitchen. The night was cool but clear. The drizzle had vanished. We could hear the sea at the bottom of the cliff.

"You hear, Philippa? The sea just crashes and crashes. That's what waves do. That is their ambition, what they were born for."

"And with us?" I was dying to know.

"With us, we're born, we reproduce and we die. All this," he spread his arms around him, "is *samsara*."

Charming.

"There, you're doing it again!" he said.

"What?"

"You keep quiet, you shut yourself off. Why not say what you're thinking?"

"No one would like me if I did that. It's more than my life is worth."

I kicked a stone from the pathway and had the pleasure of watching it disappear over the cliff. Power.

"You've had a very sad time. It will end when your

body dies. But your mind will never die. You must look after it, so that your next reincarnation is on a higher plane. Now is opportunity to gain enlightenment."

Terrific. Though perhaps it was best to know the truth. I had lived in hope that tomorrow would be better. Not necessarily so.

We left the dishes to soak and Mighoal offered to escort me to my chalet. I expected him to disappear then, but he followed me, stayed to have cheese and crackers at the communal table; no sign of him yawning or disappearing to a chanting session. When I went to the bedroom to fetch a hankie, he came too, stretched himself on the bed, fixed his limpid eyes on me, then reached towards me with his soft, full, moist lips that tasted of Tibetan glaciers and spring sunshine. Or perhaps the Camembert was particularly good. I'd been reading about Tibetan life, love and the pursuit of happiness, how "Tibetans treat the sexual act with the same sense of enjoyment as that of a good meal." No strings attached. Bliss. But what happens if you got fond of the buggers? Pudding too, I suppose.

"Oh, Buddha!" She-of-the-snoring husband burst into the room. "Won't be a mo. Then you can carry on!"

Mighoal took my hand and indicated the door. Obediently, I followed.

"It's all yours," I said to she-of-the-snoring husband as we left the chalet.

We retraced our steps down the shingle path, through clumps of gorse, till we came to a row of single-storey wooden huts. We entered the first of these. There was a mat on the floor, a wood stove, a wok on a camping gas cylinder, and a kettle surrounded by tin mugs.

"Our needs are so simple," I said to Mig. "Shelter, food and heat."

"Yes. In Tibet, if we have all three, we're satisfied. Though, even without them, people are still happy. They know unhappiness is just a feeling; it will pass. The spring will come, the soil will heat and crops will grow. In the west, even with everything, people are very, very unhappy. A problem of the spirit."

"Though sometimes it's the body." I sank to my knees in agony.

"You ill?" Mig asked.

"Baby. Feels like it wants out. But it mustn't."

"Lie. On the mat."

He bundled his jacket into a pillow and placed my head on top. He disappeared and returned with a blanket.

"Will I get a doctor?"

"I don't know. The pain has stopped. Maybe it'll be OK."

Mig put his hands on my tummy. "Yes, maybe. Once you've rested."

As a child, I used to think if you wanted something to come true badly enough, then it would.

"How old?"

"Ten whole weeks."

Mig's face looked so sad, I felt a little better. It was

nice to feel someone cared, someone was worrying too. He sat cross-legged, took my hand and let out a low rumbling grief-like noise.

"Sometimes it takes a while for a baby to settle down in the womb." I tried to reassure myself, knowing that if the baby didn't want to stay, nothing on earth could be done to make it.

He looked at me and smiled. Another pain. He put his arms around me. I felt strange being held by someone in priestly garb, awesome, holy. And he smelt of cloth and incense.

By midnight, there was blood. Bright red.

"Not a good sign." My tears made me feel something awful was going to happen.

At two o'clock there was a raw, knife-sharp pain, lots of blood.

"I think, Philippa, I must get a doctor."

"It's too late for that. Anyway, there's nothing you can do. I remember a friend losing a baby, too. She tried everything: hormones, 'bed rest', gentle music, she even went to Mass."

He made tea and poured something out of a bottle into it.

"This might help. Will it be painful? I could get you medicine."

I was past caring. One pain heaped on another didn't seem to make much difference.

I screamed. Mig jumped up as if bitten by a snake and fled. Then, I really let it rip. Yelled and screamed some more. Shouted obscenities, cursed the fates.

A battalion of monks came through the door. Half a dozen, anyway. They gibbered amongst themselves, seemed cross with Mig, pointed at me, then at the room. One of them ran to give the fire a jizz up; another put the kettle on. An older, bald fellow with twinkling eyes came to me and knelt by my side. He put a cool hand to my head.

"No fever. That is good. You must watch for infection, so there will be more babies."

"You must be joking!" I sobbed. "I just want to die."

"Don't worry – when the time comes for that to happen, that's when you'll want to live more than ever!"

A real charmer.

The evening then became quite cosy. Mig took up his spot beside me, unabashed. The rest sat in a circle, yammering ninety to the dozen in jungle sounds, drinking tea laced with whatever was in Mig's bottle. Those with bald heads shone like beacons, while those with hair had it glued to their forehead with sweat.

Just as I was drifting off, another knife-like pain grabbed me. I curled into a ball, had an urge to get up. Mig tried to stop me. The room was suddenly quiet. Overtaken by something I couldn't resist, I squatted and, in front of the riveted gathering, at the end of a long scream of pain when it felt as though my insides were splitting apart, a tiny bundle lay on the mat. A big head, two arms and two legs. Lifeless. I lay back. Relieved. It was over. And I was OK.

Mig looked at it with a mixture of disbelief and wonder.

"So tiny." He cradled it in a tissue and laid it beside me. It was Jack and me and both of us together, finished. Nothing left now but memories.

Mig made tea, lifted my head to give me a sip.

"You will have many, many babies. This little one was not perfect. Nature is wisest."

But cruel.

"What were you going to call the little baby?"

Just baby.

"Try to speak about it, tell me what your hopes were."

"I thought baby and me would live happily ever after in a nice little farm at the edge of a mountain."

"Yes, it's better to cry, or you can scream here if you want to. Nobody minds. They understand."

They had returned to their gossiping and tea drinking.

"Your mountain sounds nice. We have nothing but mountains in Tibet. But the Chinese are making big roads all over them, bringing in more people. The old ways are gone, the monasteries destroyed. You cannot destroy the spirit, it lives on and on. Your little baby will have a reincarnation, a new life as something else."

All I could see was a tiny dead body.

"Was it a boy or a girl?" I asked.

He held the bundle in the palm of his hand near the light.

"A girl." He smiled. "I have a feeling she will have a happy reincarnation – a bird, a beautiful fish, maybe."

Somehow, I was consoled. She wasn't totally lost.

One of the group said something to Mig. He turned to me.

"They want to know if you'd like to cremate the body. They would say the prayers for the dead for you, and you could keep the ashes in a special box."

The idea of burning horrified me. "No, don't burn her. I'd rather she were buried."

"And the prayers?"

"Yes, I'd like those for her, for Juno." Goddess of marriage and childbirth, two things she would never experience.

Mig passed her to the first in the group, speaking her name. He chanted something which included the name, and passed her on to his neighbour, who did the same.

The room now seemed different, full somehow, no shadows. I felt Jack there too, around, happy. At least he'd said he'd been happiest with me.

They handed Juno back to me. Someone had placed her in a wooden box with a carved lid.

"It's for holding sacred things," Mig said.

Unbelievably, I felt happy. We were all the same. Juno went first and the rest of us would follow, sometime.

I thanked all of them for their prayers and their consolation.

"We are pleased to be here with you," one of them said. "Death teaches us the seriousness of life."

They wished us a good night and filed out the door.

Mig put more wood on the fire and lay beside me on the mat. Juno lay in her box on the other side.

"Tomorrow we'll find a place for her to rest," I said.

The morning sun had burnt the mist away, though there was a stiff breeze down the cliff. We went in search of a fuchsia – its blossom reminds me of ballerinas, with purple tutu and long, slim legs. Mig brought a terracotta pot, put some sand in the bottom and nodded at my little bundle.

I opened the wooden box, drew back the tissue covering. There she was, no bigger than an apple, large, round head bent into a tiny body, toy arms held together.

"You are what might have been. And now you'll never feel the warm sun on your back, the wind in your hair, my arms around you, Jack's love within you."

Mig let the tears roll down his cheeks and the snot drip from his nose.

I held my unformed baby, told her how much she meant to me, how much I loved Jack, that she was part of that love between us. I placed her halfway down the pot, Mig lifted the fuchsia and spread its roots around. He filled it with soil.

In spite of myself, I cried. And cried.

"That's my daughter there, Mig. Do you understand?"

He nodded. Squeezed my hand. "I can understand."

"She will be well looked after here."

"You're a kind person, Mig. I could have done with you weeks ago. Anyway, you're here now. Except, if you'll excuse me, I need to go and lie down." I was feeling suddenly weak and exhausted.

He opened the door to the chalet and kissed me goodbye.

She of the snoring husband was sitting reading.

"Like to borrow it?" she asked, offering me a thick book with a spider pouring blood on the cover. "Most enjoyable thing I've read for ages. Could do with a book like that every month."

She must have seen my face.

"Sorry – you OK?"

"Had a bit of a difficult night. Lost my baby."

"God, no! What age was it?"

"Ten weeks."

"Cot death?"

"Miscarriage."

"A *miscarriage* at ten weeks! Sure, that wasn't a baby, that was only a twinkle in its daddy's eye. About the size of a grape. I'd a few of them myself. It's only a baby at thirty weeks, when it has all its bits and pieces and can stay alive itself."

I passed on into the bedroom and locked the door.

It was dark when Mig brought me supper – the remains of a bean stew and lamb kebabs with yoghurt sauce.

"Specially for you," he said.

His presence seemed to fill the room, envelope me

with cords of strength. All he had to do was look at me and I felt better.

"How do you do that?" I asked him. He looked puzzled. "Create a feeling of such comfort and hope."

"I feel a strong human feeling for you. I sympathise with your suffering, with your loss, your hopes and dreams. You are learning that nothing is permanent, everything is in a state of change. What we always do is try to cling to what we think are certainties. There are none."

"No guarantees. All the same, I have to do something with my life. I can't go back to what I've been doing, with those people: Bonkers, Henry and Eddie, not to mention Constantia of the big teeth. I realise now that that life held nothing of importance. *Nineteenth century realism* or *twentieth century expressionism* seem a totally crazy pursuit, after what's happened to me. Reality is now. Being human – not poring over a collection of paintings or shelves of books."

"You have learnt a lot, Philippa. You could stay here, join us on a year's retreat."

He lay back on the bed. "But I think perhaps you ought to face what you are leaving behind, go back and complete all those loose ends."

"Face Bonkers *et al*!"

He looked at me steadily. "Yes, I really think so."

I thought about it for ten seconds.

"I suppose you're right. Not to would be running away. I want to run *to* something. Make a living the best way I know how, in a way that helps me to make peace with myself. Jack found his way in Provence. It was lovely – except for the goats and Dorrie and Ast. But the idea of being alone, having to fend for myself, that's OK."

He nodded, took my plate and put it on the floor. Then sat beside me and put his arm around me.

"If you need any help, I will do what I can."

A knot of hope and anxiety in my stomach.

"I don't think I'll make any plans, ever again."

"Plans are good fun, so long as you don't expect them to turn out the way you planned them! Slowly, imperceptibly things alter till, one day, the beat of a butterfly's wing in Kerry can cause an earthquake in China!"

That must have been what Jack meant when he said our union would shatter the icecap.

I must have fallen asleep. The last thing I remember was melting glaciers, giant waves pouring down from the Arctic, yet I felt warm and unconcerned.

Chapter Thirteen

❧

A merry heart goes all the day

Mighoal waited for me outside the door the day I left the spur of rock jutting into the Atlantic. In the early morning light he looked about sixteen but he was easily twice that. "Must be pure living," I'd said to him. "Your face hasn't even a ghost of a crease and you've got all your teeth."

"No sugar," he said. "In Tibet, it's lucky to get food."

We walked down the shale path, past the meditation room. I hate leave-takings, the finality of them. I tried to pretend my departure was a day trip, that I'd be back.

"Juno – the plant – you wish to take her?"

"No, not now. I've nowhere to put her, just yet."

We got to Limerick in a couple of hours, drank some tea from my flask and took the train for Dublin. Mighoal seemed like a piece of moss landed on my skin, a comforting presence, a bright candle on a dark night. He was to stay with me before leaving for the boat to Holyhead, and then on to the Buddhist centre in France for a three-year silent retreat.

"You mean, even if your leg's hanging off you can't say a word?" I asked.

He laughed. "We're not so crazy. If it's life or death, you can speak. But the idea is to learn to be fully present, not thinking about yesterday, what you're going to talk about next, what you're going to do tonight."

"The number of times I plan dinner in my head, then make lists of what I need to buy, then work out the time I need to be home in order to have it to eat at seven. Sometimes, I even think about the following day's meal, so that I can cook it that night and not have to worry what's for dinner two days ahead."

He nodded. "So, you see, it stops you thinking about death."

In that case, all this thinking is very worthwhile.

"Who wants to think about that?" I enquired.

"It's the most important thing in life," he said, his face solemn as an empty church.

Peaches and Feelya had left the mews spick and span for my return, even the pot plants were shining. The fridge was stocked with three varieties of pizza – that Italian abomination, full of pesticide-ridden tomatoes. I wondered if poodles like pizza. They probably don't live long enough for the chemicals to do them much damage.

Mig made a beeline for the bamboo bed. I told him

it was dicey after the depredations of Peaches and Ophelia. He examined it thoroughly, said it was OK except that the bamboo had dried out too much and needed a good soaking, and the headboard had a family of woodworm burrowing to their hearts' content.

He settled for the futon and I promised to water the bed.

We had a hot whiskey apiece while I prepared something to eat.

"Steak-and-kidney pudding?" I asked. Miggie assented.

"I say before, Tibetans eat meat," he said, "though we respect animals."

"That's a slight contradiction," I said, tossing the kidney into the seasoned flour. I always use suet and steam the whole lot. Unbelievable flavour, though nowadays few bother.

"Not at all!" he said. "We never kill animals ourselves, never go hunting, so there is no blood on our hands. We believe in the equality of all that lives."

Sounded like a bit of a cop-out, getting someone else to do your dirty work. My silence must have said a multitude.

"If there is no one to slaughter, then one person is assigned to it. It would not be right to let children starve."

Amen to that.

For pudding, I knocked up a Swiss roll with rose-flavoured butter filling. All the while sipping my hot whiskey, heavy with cloves and lemon. I felt almost delighted to be alive, though still with the heaviness that Jack and Juno were no more.

"Care to come out and see the fish?" I put the dried *Daphnia* into my pocket and topped up our glasses.

It was warm and still outside, midges hopped in the air, the roses dripped petals. I pulled the net off the pond and, with a stick, dragged some of the weed to the edge to give the fish more oxygen.

There were only two left, skulking about at the bottom where it was warmer. Mig ruffled the water and they came to the surface, mouths wide for food. I tossed them some of the dried specks.

"For the Chinese fish are lucky, a sign of a long life. That's why they eat so many. The Chinese are stupid."

"That's very unspacious of you, Mig."

"With the Chinese, it's different."

That's what we all say, whether it's chinks or tinks or magazine editors; just depends who's annoying us at the time.

Violet came rushing towards us. "You're back! We could smell the dinner wafting up the garden. I said to George, that's definitely Miss Woodpeck's cooking. The two ladies only ever used the microwave."

I introduced my pet Tibetan, who gave her a reverential bow. She rose to the occasion, licked a finger and smoothed an eyebrow. I was beginning to feel ill.

"By the way, George, em . . ."

Don't tell me – he'd caught pneumonia guddling in the bucket in the windy garden . . .

"That is, Georgie and me, we'd like to say how sorry we are for your trouble – your friend getting killed with blood-poisoning and all that. Terrible to-do. And you a suspect! I *had* to tell Dolly, of course, in case the American papers got hold of it and Dolly's address coming into disrespect – you know what I mean. Your sister very kindly filled us in on *all* the details."

Good old Aggie. I wondered how long it would take a couple of goldfish to dispose of a corpse.

Violet stood about for an eternity, hopping from one varicose-veined leg to another, flashing her eyes at Mig and clacking her false teeth at me. She would have to torture me even harder to get any more information. A bell ringing in the distance sent her scurrying.

"That'll be Georgie! Can't bear to have me out of his sight for five minutes. Time for his cocoa."

Mig raised an eyebrow as she sped down the garden. "Now, Philippa, *your* turn to be a little spacious."

"Do you really want to eat tonight?"

Barely had the gravy been mopped and the last of the second glass of wine sipped when there was a scuffle outside.

I put my finger to my lips and tiptoed towards the lamp to turn it off.

"Philippa? That you? I know you're there, 'cos Violet phoned me."

I gestured to Mig to open the door while I poured the last of the wine into my glass.

Ag didn't so much enter as flurried into the room.

"You look as though you've just come through a very thorny hedge," I said.

She looked at me and then came to sit beside me.

"How've you been? I was worried about you."

"Worried? So worried, you told the talking newspaper below all my business! Is there nothing sacred?"

Her shoulders collapsed in on her. She took out a ball of tissue and blew her nose. Just what I needed – an attack of the weepies. Mig sat on the floor in his meditation pose, offering it all up.

"Bring on the can-can girls, let's have a real circus!" I got up to rummage for another bottle of wine. Only a Chardonnay left. The colour of horse piss and tasting of something terminal. Aggie stopped the tears and looked at me with her little sad mouth. What the hell! I brought her a glass.

She got up and flung her arms around me. "Gosh, Philly, if you only knew how I care about you."

"You've a very peculiar way of showing it, sister."

"But I didn't tell her a word about the baby. Not a word."

"Just as well. It's gone."

She sat down again, eyes wild. "Gone? Where?"

I pointed to the heavens.

"Oh, God!" And that was the last Aggie spoke all evening. Between her sobs and Mig's chanting, I'd a whale of a time. Perhaps I should have cried too, but I was too numb. Just yet. Besides, there was a bottle of wine to finish.

I woke early, with half a brain. The other part was trying to disentangle itself and making a painful fist of it. Mig was still in his meditation pose, though silent, staring into space at the usual 45° angle. He could stay like that for days at a time, not even needing to go to the loo.

Aggie lay curled up on the couch, folded hands cradling her face, defenceless, barely breathing. I felt tenderness for her like that; awake and talking, she set my teeth on edge. Someone once told me it's the parts of *ourselves* we see in other people that we dislike, and so blame others for our own faults and failings.

Ag heard me thinking; she opened an eye, fixed it on me, closed it again and turned the other way.

I put the kettle on and thought about something cheerful, like death. That's when Mig came to. Gentle as a butterfly, he came towards me, gave me a big hug and smiled.

"Coffee or tea?" I asked.

He settled for coffee and a cheese and jam sandwich.

"You know, Mig, the world's a funny place. There's Aggie. Unhappy as a swallow in a winter storm. There's only the two of us – we've a brother in Australia, but we don't ever talk about him – and yet we can't seem to . . . you know, *connect*. We seem to spark off one another when we ought to be helping each other to be happy, to be cheerful."

The cheese and jam lying on the white bread

looked like blood seeping from wounded flesh. Give me a bit of live food any day – lettuce and onion, even. Mig was grateful for it, all the same.

"Your jam is – *extra*, as the French say. To be honest, I hate going there, to the retreat house in the Auvergne. I heard it is hard. The nearest village is ten miles. Nothing but rock, and more rock."

"You, like the rest of us, have a choice. You could languish in front of a television set, go for a pint with the lads once a week to tell them how the world should be run, spend the next day or two recovering and start the whole thing all over again the following week."

He wiped the crumbs from his mouth, fixed his large, brown eyes on me. "That is worse than anything! That is truly *samsara* – without relief. No spiritual food."

He stared dreamily into space while I made another sandwich.

"You know, Philippa, if people were to turn off the television, sit with that silence, then there might be something."

"Speaking of silence, one of Ag's magazines had a very interesting advert for a farm. A tiny one, mind you. Cheap too, on account of it being in the mountains; 'the oldest ones in the country', it said; rounded and smooth. The Slieve Blooms. I like the name – the 'blooming' mountains. I might just be able to scrabble enough money together to buy it."

Ag stirred. "I saw that ad too. I even saw the farm – *very* run-down. Best thing to do would be knock down the whole lot and build on the site."

Mig raised an eyebrow. "We'll see it, anyway – tomorrow?"

"What about your retreat house in the Auvergne?" I asked.

Mig bit into another piece of oozing flesh. "That can wait," he said, which worried me even more. Why was he with me? What did he want?

It wasn't the best day to begin a search for anything, except misery. Ag had a stiff gin for breakfast, felt "woozy" and collapsed on to the bed. I made a sandwich for her lunch and locked the cocktail cabinet.

"We've some problems in Tibet with *chang*; some drink too much, especially the Sherpas, to protect themselves against the cold."

"At least it's fairly pure. It's the chemicals they don't tell you about in gin that cause all the trouble. Ravage the brain. That's why I stick to wine," I said.

He looked at me as though I were normal.

I asked him to carry the bag with the bottles and glasses, and I carried the one with the roast beef sandwiches smeared with horseradish sauce. Lemon tart to follow. In the wilds of the Slieve Blooms, there might not even be a tea shop.

However, there was. One. A cosy sitting-room, with stuffed animals and hairy jumpers for sale. Hot tea bursting from the pot and warm sultana scones. Mig had a second, piled with raspberry jam.

"You'll have no teeth left by the time you get to France."

"Did you ever think I may not need them? There is fasting too, you know. No jam."

The tea shop lady let us leave our bags while we went in search of Doatens Kelly's farm.

"She's moving into Mrs Fierty's home in Ballinamore," we were informed. "A grand place. Three meals a day, an outing once a week and a hairdresser'll come to your own *room*, if you want. You've to pay extra for a view. Five pounds a week extra. Anyway, all the views are taken. Doatens has her name down for when someone kicks . . . you know, leaves permanent-like."

We climbed the tiny track up the mountain, where we were to turn left when we saw the ducks, carry on till we saw the big lilac, the farm was on the right. Doatens was "certain to be there. She'd goats to milk and eggs to collect."

The sort of place a bird doesn't hop but the entire neighbourhood is out counting its feathers.

The air was thinner; Miggie, quite a bit behind me, practised his walking meditation. The swallows hung high in the air, then suddenly swooped, bent their rubber bodies, raced around me and then back up again into the clear, blue sky.

The track suddenly levelled out and I stood still. The midland plains stretched to pale blue at the horizon, punctured by one or two hills and chimneys with strings of smoke. Not an exciting landscape, none of the drama of Provence. Perhaps this was the right place, after all.

Speaking of which, Mig caught up with me, his brown eyes almost dripping down to his chin.

"How on earth do you manage to make your eyes your entire face? I know they're supposed to be the mirror of the soul, but yours go overboard."

"There is always that little remark, like the thorn in the rose. It takes you by surprise."

"Sorry! No offence meant."

It was fear that did it, but that was too difficult to explain. He could make what he liked of me, I hadn't the energy to stand up for myself; to tell him how, really, I was OK, it was just the scaffolding that was a little faulty.

We looked about for our next marker, and there it was at the bottom of the track.

"It's the lilac," I said, "I'd know it anywhere. Nellie had one on the Blaskets at her mother's house. She wore the colour all her life, she even dyed her shoes a pale mauve."

"In Tibet, it is a mystical colour; if you prefer violet, you desire a mystical union."

"That would make sense. Nellie wanted nothing but perfection in men, so she never married. Her illusions are still intact, she still thinks Mr Wonderful is out there looking for her."

"And Philippa? What colour does she like?"

"Let's go and meet Doatens." I'd no desire to be hanged, drawn and quartered.

The cottage nestled at the bottom of the track, surrounded by stone walls and sheltered by an enormous beech tree. The lilac was in full bloom and humming with bees.

Doatens was in the yard, tossing food to the hens. "Come on, girls, grab what ye can, ye'll not get a second chance. That's it, Hetty, don't take any nonsense from that sister of yours, Miss High and Mighty, thinks she can rule the yard just because old cock-a-doodle-do has taken a fancy to her on account of her silky feathers and fancy comb. You're just as good-looking, only not as snooty. So what if you're a bit bedraggled like myself, after all these years, working hard. Anyone'd grow a beard. That old bitch of a nurse, telling me I'd have to get it off with needles! A beard never did anyone any harm. Saves the need of a scarf . . ."

She stopped when I started to giggle. A toothless grin followed the silence.

"I've . . . we've come to see the farm," I said.

She scattered the rest of the grain to the hens, put down the bowl, and came towards us.

"Foreign, you are," she said to Mig. He did his eye-droop routine.

"Tibet," he answered.

"'Next door to heaven', so I heard on the radio. Full of monks, Sherpas and fellows trying to climb mountains. Plenty of mountains around here but no one bothers. Come in and rest yourselves." She looked steadily at me, counting my feathers, examining the cut of my comb. A large black cat sat on the doorstep, daring us to enter. He looked straight into my soul, got up and rubbed himself against my leg.

"Mr Perkins likes you, anyways," said Doatens.

Mr Perkins slunk off, scattering the hens as he went.

Inside, a kettle steamed on top of a tiny yellow range with *Cleopatra* on the side. Promises of rare delicacies from the cook herself or her oven? She threw a good pinch of tea leaves into a shiny aluminium teapot. The connection between Alzheimer's and aluminium obviously hadn't penetrated the Slieve Blooms. I decided against letting her know.

"We let it brew in these parts." She grinned at Mig. "And, like them Sherpas, we put a bit of a taste into it betimes."

We all looked at the half-empty bottle of Powers'. As if encouraged, she poured a "decent sup" into each cup.

"Get that down ye as the tea's brewing."

She carved three slices of thick, warm brown bread, laid them side by side on a willow pattern plate. The table already had a dish of butter and a pot of honey.

Dark brown tea, made with mountain spring water, nutty brown bread thick with butter and honey. She had the second slice ready just as we finished the first.

"Used to make me own butter. But the old fingers gave out when Betsy went dry in the autumn. Honey's Mr Pim's – from the knapweed; best taste on earth. Quakers are kind to their bees."

She looked steadily at me. "You'll be wanting to make friends with him."

I felt like kissing her, but restrained myself. I'd a feeling Doatens had her pride.

"There's been many a one looking at my little farm. Tall ones, with small minds; small ones with big ideas. Not a smidgen of wit between them all. Told everyone it was gone. Sold. You look as if you'd just *love* it. Like I do. Every nook and cranny, every cranesbill and cowslip."

She dabbed her eyes with the bottom of her apron.

"And why do you have to leave your home?" Mig asked. I got up to pour her more tea.

"I'm not able any more. Winters are bad. I'm stuck here because of that ridge you came past. It gets twenty feet high with snow and no one can get past in a car. Some come through by walking and climbing. The flu got me one winter too many, last time. It's time to go. Still, the home in the town has a telly and company, if I want. And all the cooking done for me. You see, I have a few little problems with this and that. Best thing is to be near a hospital."

"Wouldn't you like to die here?" Mig persisted.

"Yes and no. I'm not much looking forward to dying, wherever it happens. But I'd prefer to be cosy and snug and just fade away, than be dragged into a stupor with cold."

"I've just buried someone. Someone close," I found myself confessing.

"I could tell you'd been through the wars. Rings under your eyes. A mouth that hasn't smiled in ages. Plenty here to keep your mind off your troubles.

Seventy-two acres, though some of that is scrub and moorland, but a few good fields in the lower bit. PJ next door is always trying to wean them from me. The things that man has promised me if only I'd sell them! But where would I be going on a holiday to America? Not many people get back alive. One killed every second. And PJ *hates* goats. Nanny'd be the first to go. He can't abide her, says I have her spoilt, overfed. Just because I give her the odd bit of scone and butter. I hope you like goats."

"Well, to be truthful, Miss Kelly, we had three contrary ones in France."

"Ah, them Frenchies is all the same. Nanny's a sound Irish goat. You'll love her. A real lady. Has a soft spot for an apple. Milk her twice a day when she's in full flush and then once a day when the kids need more."

I could hardly wait.

"They mostly have twins."

Of course. I wouldn't have it any other way.

"And then there's my little brown cow, a Dexter. Bit temperamental when she's calved but the best mother going. Buckets of thick, creamy milk. I used make the butter with her milk, scones and bread with the buttermilk. Nanny's milk used feed the pigs but I got out of them. Couldn't raise the bacon in the chimney to smoke it with the creaking in me bones. So the kids get it all now but you could make that queer stuff – yowgurt. Mash it up with a few raspberries that grow wild on the sides of the moorland, bit of sugar. Grand, I'm sure. Bit sour but . . ."

A car rumbling down the track stopped her in mid-speak. She was out the door in seconds. And back in again.

"It's him. The one who's desperate to get me little farm. No, no. You two stay put, back me up."

She opened the door of the range and threw in a few sods of turf and fistful of twigs. The car had stopped in the yard. A door opened and banged shut. Doatens filled the kettle from a bucket of clear water and put in on to the range.

A long black shadow stood on the doorstep. Doatens hung her head to one side, screwed up her mouth and eyes as if she were trying to make sense of the world.

"Who goes there?" she asked the shadow in a creepy voice.

"Just me, back," said a very posh, un-Irish voice. "I've been to the planning people and everything seems normal. So, I phoned my solicitor who has given the OK."

Doatens now looked the picture of a demented camel, complete with overshot jaw. "As I says to yez afore, many hundreds are interested in my little farm. I'd had viewers by the dozen this last while. But these good people here were the first and they're settled on it. The deposit's in the post."

"No problem, Miss Kelly," the talking shadow said, "I can give you the whole amount now, in cash."

The voice came towards the table and drew a huge wad of money from an inside pocket and began to dole it out. Close up, Shadow didn't look too bad. Large brown eyes, large brown curls, pale pink lips in a curving mouth. I couldn't quite see his teeth.

"Fifty, one hundred, one hundred and fifty, two hundred . . . "

"Ye can stop right there!" Doatens dropped her crazy old lady act and became Lady Bracknell with a Slieve Bloom accent. "I've given my word and that's that. The farm goes to . . . this lady here."

Shadow looked steadily at me. "With all due respect, Miss Kelly, your lady here looks as though lifting a bird's nest would be a day's work, never mind chasing sheep halfway up a mountain, or even milking your precious Nanny! Besides, we had an understanding. A gentleman's agreement."

"Well, I'm no gintleman," said Doatens, "so put that in yer pipe and smoke it."

Shadow slowly gathered the money, folded it and put it back into his pocket. You could have heard a hair split. I desperately wanted to cough.

"An agreement was made, Miss Kelly – and I'm going to see that it's kept!"

We waited till the engine whined down the hill before we breathed. Even Mig had one or two beads of sweat on his brow.

"Wow!" he said. "I've met a snow leopard in broad daylight but never anything so frightening as that."

"All guff, if you ask me," said Doatens. "That fella couldn't fight his way out of a paper bag."

She sat down all the same and didn't refuse my offer

to make more tea. I undid the picnic and offered her a sandwich. She opened it to check, sniffed it and took a bite. It disappeared in seconds.

"That's a grand sandwich, though the beef isn't home-reared. You can tell *that* easy."

We looked at her.

"Nothing surer than the taste of grass. That animal only ever ate bag feed."

However, the lemon tart disappeared without comment, except that it merited a "tiny bit of sloe gin".

Unfortunately for the rest of my life, the sloe gin was out of this world. I got the recipe from her there and then.

"The bushes all the way down to the valley below are blackthorn – a mass of white froth in the springtime, and solid blue-black berries before Christmas. Don't pick them too early, mind. They're best when the frost's been at them."

I wrote that down too.

After our third top-up, Doatens's face became red with anxiety.

"Do you think now, Philippa, that golliwog of a fella will make trouble? I'm trying hard not to think about it but it's like trying to keep a bull from a cow in heat, just can't be done."

I looked at Mig for a little help but all I got was his 45 degree angle and a look that said "*samsara*" and "let's be spacious". So, it was back to me.

"Well, one way to find out is to go to the solicitor and get him to draw up a contract between you and me. That should fix him."

Doatens' solicitor was a bit like herself, charming and frail and about a hundred and fifty years old.

He looked as though he ate dust for breakfast. A bony hand pressed mine, Mig got a nod, and we were given a tot of whiskey apiece. Mr Crawley begged us to be seated amongst his heaps of yellowed papers and sun-bleached law tomes.

His appearance belied his efficiency. He had the papers drawn up on his laptop, the sealing-wax melted and the seal pressed firmly into it inside twenty minutes.

Doatens explained that she'd decided to sell the farm to me, as she liked the cut of my "jib" and I'd had experience of death in the south of France. The old man nodded as if nothing could be more felicitous. I was as puzzled as Mig.

"When you live near to the land like I've done, Philippa – and you'll be doing yourself, shortly – you have to know that life has an end, like your poor friend found in the south of France. He's up above now, rearing cucumbers for the almighty and his cohorts. That's what it was all about – becoming a vegetable farmer, so he could be useful when he went beyond."

It was a nice thought, but . . .

"Well, to be honest, Doatens, I'd have preferred him to grow cucumbers for us and our children and our grandchildren. I'm sure Jack was the last person to know he was doing it all according to some grand plan."

"But that's the trick of it all! We just don't know, and you look the type who's been through the mill and is ready at a young age to learn what it's all about. Death."

"I was sort of hoping there would be something in-between."

"Don't get me wrong, now, there is something in-between, something very important. But it's only death that learns it to us. And that's the value of life. The chance we have to do a bit of good, be kind, love animals."

Mr Crawley accepted a £10 note from me as a "down payment", and I gave my word I'd have the balance for him as soon as I could. Doatens and I signed the contract over another sloe gin. Mr Crowley handed each of us a copy and bade us farewell. He said if there was ever anything he could do for me, only say the word . . .

Later, in the local hostelry, Mig bent towards me.

"What Doatens was saying, it's what I've been telling to you for all the time. This life is a chance to get *karma*, save it up so our next incarnation is more joyful."

Sounded absolutely *wonderful*, I could hardly wait. I restrained myself from leaping up and away on the next train. But I'd a delicious cup of tea to finish, the best I'd had since Nelly stopped getting her special sachets from her nieces in America.

Doatens drained her second glass of Irish coffee,

collecting the cream with her finger and making noisy licking sounds.

"Well, my God!" she said in mid-lick. "Would you look who it is."

Golliwog, with a stranger.

"That's young Sweeney he's with. A bit of a fly boy, trying to make his mark as one of them whizzy lawyers. Heard a few stories about him from PJ. I wonder what they're up to?"

Several days later, we found out. A long brown envelope thumped on to my floor. A letter signed by Mr Sweeney, LLB informing me that my "claim" to *Lilac Cottage* was null and void, as a prior claim existed in the person of Jonathan Todd-Hunter owing to the "witnessed" verbal agreement of the owner of *Lilac Cottage*, Miss Doatens Kelly, *aka* "Doatey K". There was a map enclosed and a three-page "Agreement" which I was to sign "forthwith" and return. It stated that I never had, and never would, press for any claim to *Lilac Cottage*, though it took three pages to say it.

The phone rang. Aggie. "What's this I hear about you and *Lilac Cottage*? Jonathan says you're trying to wrestle it away from him."

Jonathan?

"How could you do such a thing, Philippa? My own sister. I felt so embarrassed when he told me the name of the person who was trying to pull a fast one. I pretended it was another branch of the family."

Silence.

"Are you there, Philippa? I think I deserve an

explanation; after all, it was me who told you about the cottage. I wouldn't mind but it's Jonathan's dream come true. He's going to build a luxury hotel on the site, have walking tours of the mountains and run botanical weekends. He's put everything into it!"

"Look, Agatha, I'd no idea you were involved with that golliwog of a cheat. For a start, the farm was Miss Kelly's to sell, not Mr Todd-Hunter's to buy, and she decided to sell it to me. That's all there is to it."

"This isn't the end of this, Philippa. Jonathan's determined to buy that place. He's promised me the contract for the hotel interior. I've done a lot of work on it already. It's cost me a trip to see the William Morris exhibition *and* the price of the catalogue."

"I'm sure it'll all come in highly useful one day. Nothing's ever lost."

"Trust you to make philosophical arguments about deceitfulness. I really feel sorry for you over this Jack and baby business and all that, but this is different!"

Strange how everything is "different" when our own interests are at stake. I used to think Aggie had a screw loose. Now I realised she was just like any old human.

I cradled the phone as spaciously as I could without cracking the plastic and went to tell Mig all about it. There was a splash as soon as I opened the back door. He had finally done it and joined the fish.

I dragged him to dry land, still alive, but gasping.

"Perhaps you ought to learn to meditate in a safe zone," I suggested.

"I don't worry," he coughed. "I was at one with them, down there. They're bored!"

I replaced the net and stood up. It was a relief to know that even goldfish have their problems.

"Perhaps your next incarnation will be as a fish."

That sobered him up. "I better begin to build my karma, go on my retreat."

"Sorry – I didn't mean to chase you away . . ."

Especially when I'd got used to having you around, when I'd plans for you to dig me a little vegetable patch in the Slieve Blooms . . .

"It's been coming along like that, the feeling to go. The fish put what you call your 'tin lid on it'."

And, just like that, he was gone. The shadow that sat on my shoulder for weeks suddenly vanished, clutching a plastic bag with a change of clothes and some pittas filled with lettuce. He refused the poached salmon.

"How could I eat my next incarnation?" His beautiful brown eyes drooped.

I put it aside to feed to a stray cat and womanfully chewed a few lettuce leaves to death.

I hardly slept that night. Mig's absence added to other losses. The farm on Slieve Bloom seemed more important than ever and yet I knew that to want something desperately was a sure way of not getting it. So, I put it out of my mind, only to have the scent of lilac, the clucking of hens, come flooding back. At about three in the morning, I tore up Mr Todd-Hunter's agreement, set fire to the pieces and swallowed a stiff brandy. I was asleep in minutes.

The morning brought Agatha ready to do battle. Bright red lipstick slashed her mouth; rouge sat on her white cheeks like consumption marks. She'd obviously slept as little as I had.

She burst into tears. I let her in, put her on a chair and put the kettle on.

"You've no idea what this means to me, Philippa," she whined.

I braced myself.

"It's to be my one big project. The jewel in my crown."

If that was all she got in her crown, she'd be lucky. Perhaps I ought to find the sticking-plaster to seal my lips.

"I've the fabric picked out for the curtains and the matching wallpaper. I'm even going to have the paint specially mixed."

Does sororocide have two r's or three?

"Now it's all ruined! Thanks to my own sister."

Just a plain old-fashioned cleaver would do as well as anything. Sharp.

"You always had everything, Philippa. Good looks, brains, everyone flapping about you. I've never had anything. This is my one chance to make my mark."

She took out a packet of tissues and dragged her sleeve across her wet nose.

This was too much. "Go take yourself and your self-pitying snivelling out of here!" I said. "You've *chosen* to feel miserable all your life and – wonder of wonders –

241

you've ended up being miserable! You had exactly the same opportunities as I've had but you ignored them, preferring to believe life had done you a foul turn. Why? So that you wouldn't have to get off your bum and make a little effort."

I was quite pleased with my psychological analysis. However, Agatha was not. Tears poured down her face and snot dripped on to her blouse.

Of course, idiot that I was, I melted. "Look, Agatha. Get it all into perspective. This Mr Todd-Hunter doesn't seem desperately straightforward. He's been up to no good with a small-time crooked solicitor. I'd wait till everything was signed and sealed before I made any more plans."

"And if it all falls through," Agatha came to, remarkably composed, "I'll only have you to blame."

Was there the merest trace of smugness? Indeed, whatever happened, it would be my fault. *Plus ça change, plus c'est la même chose.*

"Listen, Agatha! The whole bloody thing is yours! I couldn't bear your self-pity dripping all over the place as soon as I moved in. I'll find somewhere else."

Somewhere with no address, on a road that goes nowhere. Just so long as it was away from everyone. Everyone. The ones I cared about were dead.

A card from Mig:

Pips — arrived safely in Auvergne, France. Funny cattle, funny people, but Buddha's Buddha nature is

*as good as anyone else's, so must forgive that it's not
Ireland. They think here that perhaps one of my
incarnations was a leprechaun! I seek enlightenment.*

And a phone call from Doatens: "That you,
Philippa?"

I didn't like to tell her it wasn't necessary to shout
just because Slieve Bloom was a long way from Dublin.

"That Todd-Hunting man was here again. Said the
farm was as good as his. So I told him I'd set Gay Byrne
on him, and how everyone would know he was trying
to deny me the right to sell me own home to whoever I
pleased."

"How did he take that, Doatens?"

"Well, d'ye know, I kinda felt a bit sorry for him. He
looked around the yard and then across the valley at the
view and then bent down to stroke the cat – only Mr
Perkins wouldn't stand still, and he settled for Mrs. Says
I to meself, sure he can't be all bad if he likes it so much.
But then, the next minute, he offered me enough money
to choke an elephant. It's only pound notes that man
sees when he looks out his eyes. Only pound notes."

Silence.

"So, it's yours, if you still want it."

Yes, I did. But how to pay for it, that was the
question.

My bank account had exactly £64.26. I'd heard
nothing yet from the lawyer in France. My post office
savings, the grand total of £2,300. A lifetime of Prize
Bonds – one for every birthday. Several pieces of

antique furniture, too loved to be sold. And that was it. Except, of course, for my father's stamp album. He filled it from the age of 12 when he was a miserable schoolboy, just before he turned into a miserable adult. Could I part with it?

Eddie on the doorstep, behind the biggest bunch of flowers I'd ever seen.

"Here, let me help you," I suggested, as he was about to topple into the hallway.

He thrust them towards me. "For you."

I only had half a dozen vases. "How kind. To what . . ."

"Nearly a year since Mummy's demise. Just remembering that day you spent with me. It was appreciated – though not, perhaps, at the time."

We carried the bouquet like a dead body between us to the kitchen alcove and put it in the sink.

"Sorry I wasn't there when you buried the baby. Aggie told me all about it. She's been spending a lot of time with Bonkers lately. Made him a steak-and-kidney pie."

"She probably bought it in Marks & Sparks. Aggie thinks you boil an egg longer to get it softer."

"God, Pips. You never change. Always the comment."

That was a remarkably good beginning. He knew where the door was. I didn't offer coffee.

"Won't have coffee, thanks just the same. Just thought, you know, I'd like to say thanks for the . . . memory."

Christ, Eddie. Don't do this to me. I'd much rather you stayed floating about somewhere. I hate finalities.

"Sounds terminal," I managed.

"Better to have a clean slate. Finish for good. No loose ends."

"I'd the impression life was full of those. Like the sower and his seed – some germinated, some didn't, etcetera. They all still 'hung about'."

He pulled at his curls, then at his beard, and strode up and down the room like a caged panther.

"It's this hanging about you're so fond of that I can't stand. I was very cut up when you trotted off to France without a backward glance – not even a postcard. Fortunately, I've met someone very steady who's agreed to marry me. Wants children, three meals a day and several hours television a night. Perhaps you know her? Rosalind Richmond-Quinsy."

The talkative one from my seminar, with the strange opinions about *The Gleaners*.

"What's she done to her brain?"

"Says she's thoroughly fed up with it. You had given her the impression it might not be all it was cracked up to be."

How did I guess it was going to be *my* fault?

"So, her old man left her a sizeable fortune. She's using it to collect old pine, sprucing it up and flogging it on. Says it should all fit in with motherhood. Prefer the old pine actually painted, myself, but there you are. There has to be some incompatibility or life would be a bit of a bore."

When I'd closed the door on his good-bye, given the flowers a good soaking and poured myself a glass of crisp, white wine, I pondered on the madness that ever made me think that Eddie had anything engaging about him other than his tiny black curls.

I took myself and Pop's stamp album to the only stamp dealer in the city. How he hoisted his twenty stone up the five flights of stairs to the attic of the Georgian building had my imagination racing, from cranes to the notion that perhaps he never stirred from the room and lived on packets of biscuits his friends sent by carrier pigeon.

Wordlessly, he took the album, with its torn cover and loose pages. He put in his spyglass.

I wasn't offered a seat but sat down anyway. The place was remarkably clean. One entire wall was lined with dust-free frames of stamps. The other had an oil painting of a nude male, arms akimbo and slightly tumescent. I looked at Mr Stamp. He was busy searching for something in a volume of Stanley Gibbon's catalogue.

"Ah!" he said.

I almost jumped in fright.

He turned the album towards me, and then the catalogue. With a small, white stick he pointed to a triangular stamp in the album and then to one exactly the same in the catalogue. Probably a good sign. I wouldn't have put it past Pop to have invented the odd stamp.

"First one I've ever seen. In the flesh."

"Is it a good one?"

"Good? What a meaningless word for such a treasure! It is rare, much sought-after and highly prized."

"Prized", I understood. But my pride wouldn't allow me to enquire how prized.

He closed the album and handed it to me. "Thirty-five thousand pounds. No more, no less."

Two thousand more than Doatens was asking for the farm. I'd have enough left to add a bathroom.

I handed the album back to him and nodded. Without a word, he wrote a cheque for thirty-three thousand and twenty pounds – the last being "travel expenses" – and handed it to me. The writing was tiny, spidery, at odds with his twenty-stone bulk. As I left the room, he had the page open again, his spyglass out staring at the triangular piece of paper. And I used to think academics were the only crazy ones.

For some curious reason, I felt like giving him a hug. He reminded me of a child who'd just opened a lucky-bag and found his heart's desire.

Chapter Fourteen

❦

And so to Bladhma I did come

"I'd have taken thirty," Doatens whispered, as I wrote the cheque.

"You'll probably need every penny of it at Mrs Fierty's."

"Just as long as I have me few flowers and one of Mrs Perkins' kittens – when she's a mind to drop them – I'll be fine. I was never a one for these foreign places like Dublin and Galway. You'd never know what you'd pick up, though they say the shops are a dream. Give me McGahern's any day. You can have a quiet sherry when he's tying up the bacon. Best bacon in these parts, made at home by the Corrys down the road, past the bigger of the thorn trees."

Maps in the Slieve Blooms are composed of mounds, shrubs and trees.

She poured the tea made from water taken from the Silver River.

"Though PJ next door – past the mound of yellow

stones by the river – swears by that watery stuff in the supermarket. But then, I think it's something got to do with when one of the Corrys' bulls got at his prize cow."

"Isn't one bull the same as another, Doatens?"

"Not if you're breeding pure-bred Herefords and the bull's a charley."

A little like a lord and a commoner.

She put the cheque into a brown paper bag which she deposited in the bottom of the tea caddy.

"That'll go into the bank in a day or two and I'll get Mr Crawley to draw up the papers, make it official."

That should give me enough time to say my good-byes, throw a final drunken orgy, make a steak-and-kidney pie for old Bonkers. Doatens steadied herself against the table.

"You OK, Doatens?"

She rubbed her grey head. "Just a bit of a dizzy turn. When I'm down below in Ballinamore and the thicker air, it'll suit me better."

"I promise I'll call to see you and tell you what's happening."

Tears filled her sad, blue eyes. "I was sorta counting on you doing that, though I didn't like to ask." She blew her nose on her apron. "Suppose I'd best show you the few fields and all me four-legged friends."

We pulled on wellingtons, Doatens tied a scarf around her head, and said goodbye to Mr and Mrs Perkins.

The farm was built into the side of a hill which rose behind it. We took the path made for one and a very narrow donkey and climbed to the top. The valley spread before us and the hills beyond.

"That there is the wood, an ancient piece of work they tell me, with all the trees you can think of – oak, ash, sycamore, a few crab-apples, holly, of course, and then hazel, great for stakes, and my favourite in spring, the whitebeam. Underneath, all those the bluebells and primroses gladden the old bones after the winter, a few wood anemones too; the little holes you'll see dug are the squirrels after the pignuts. Devils, those same squirrels. Eat the bark of the tree and anything else they can lay their little claws on. Cheeky, too. Defiant. Mr and Mrs Badger live in the wood with their children. Aggressive creatures, badgers. Don't ever argue with one, claw your eyes out quick as look at you."

Many a two-legged animal would do that and then sit down to tea.

"Ah, there's Poppy and her calf."

A bright red cow and calf came trotting towards us, the calf's tail in the air. They stopped short with inches to spare. The cow stretched her neck, making sniffing sounds. Doatens put her hand out, palm upturned, something sitting in it. The cow inched forward and licked the palm.

"Now, Poppy, this here is Philippa Woodcock. Queer name," she said, winking at me, "but it's what she's called. She'll be here while I put me feet up for a change in Mrs Fierty's old folks' home. Never thought I'd see the day, Poppy, but there you are."

I could have sworn a tear escaped somewhere, and not just from me.

"Don't worry, Doatens, I'll look after everyone, so things will stay just the same as they were."

"That's a comfort, anyway. Poppy's a fussy imp. Won't take no for an answer and her calves are just the same."

A bit like myself, so we should all get on like a house on fire.

I wanted to hug Doatens, to tell her she should live forever, that I'd look after the farm like I would a delicate flower, but I was frightened the words would come out peculiarly, that she'd think I was too "gushing", as Aggie would say.

Doatens disappeared down the hill, wiping her eyes on her apron.

I stood on the ridge, the cow staring at me, the calf stretching this way and that, trying to summon up the courage to get nearer. Its mother bared the whites of her eyes, sniffed at me.

"Don't worry, Poppy, I wouldn't harm a single hair on that lovely red coat of yours or your little calf. Ever."

I looked down the valley, so still, unchanging. Was this it – the still point of the turning world? Is this what they mean about "peace of mind", when you connect with something outside yourself?

In that brief spell, I hadn't thought about Jack, or my little lost baby, or Aggie or Bonkers or what I was going to have for supper.

And, for some unaccountable reason, I began to cry.